ALSO BY GARTH RISK HALLBERG

City on Fire

A FIELD GUIDE TO THE
NORTH AMERICAN FAMILY

A
FIELD GUIDE
TO THE
NORTH AMERICAN
FAMILY

CONCERNING CHIEFLY THE HUNGATES AND HARRISONS, WITH
ACCOUNTS OF THEIR HABITS, NESTING, DISPERSION, ETC., AND
FULL DESCRIPTION OF THE PLUMAGE OF BOTH ADULT AND
YOUNG, WITHIN A TAXONOMIC SURVEY OF SEVERAL ASPECTS
OF DOMESTIC LIFE

BY

GARTH RISK HALLBERG

WITH SIXTY-THREE ILLUSTRATIONS DONE BY VARIOUS ARTISTS

VINTAGE

1 3 5 7 9 10 8 6 4 2

Vintage
20 Vauxhall Bridge Road,
London SW1V 2SA

Vintage is part of the Penguin Random House group of companies whose
addresses can be found at global.penguinrandomhouse.com

Penguin
Random House
UK

First published in Vintage in 2017

Originally published in slightly different form by Mark Batty Publisher,
New York, in 2007 and 2011.

The author is grateful to Buzz Poole, Christopher D. Salyers,
Cassandra J. Pappas, Oliver Munday, and all the artists who generously
contributed their time and talents—and especially to Sean Peterson.

Jacket design and endpaper art by Oliver Munday

penguin.co.uk/vintage

A CIP catalogue record for this book is available from the British Library

ISBN 9781784707446

Printed and bound in China by C&C Offset Printing Co., Ltd.

Penguin Random House is committed to a sustainable future for our business,
our readers and our planet. This book is made from Forest Stewardship
Council® certified paper.

MIX
Paper from
responsible sources
FSC® C018179

"A piece of the body torn out by the roots
might be more to the point."
                                            —James Agee

TWO REPRESENTATIVE FAMILIES

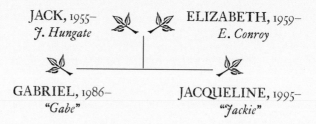

JACK, 1955–
J. Hungate

ELIZABETH, 1959–
E. Conroy

GABRIEL, 1986–
"Gabe"

JACQUELINE, 1995–
"Jackie"

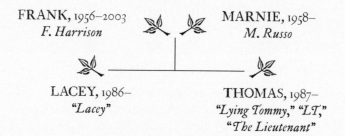

FRANK, 1956–2003
F. Harrison

MARNIE, 1958–
M. Russo

LACEY, 1986–
"Lacey"

THOMAS, 1987–
"Lying Tommy," "LT,"
"The Lieutenant"

HOW TO USE THIS BOOK

It is sincerely hoped that this novella will prove to be of value for all readers. To that end, several methods have been provided for navigation.

* *A CAPITALIZED GUIDEWORD* appears at the top of each even-numbered page, denoting that page's entry. The reader may choose to move through the entries sequentially—which is to say, alphabetically.

* PRIMARY CROSS-REFERENCES near the end of entries direct the reader to associated entries. The reader may wish to follow these cross-references until all entries have been read and the narrative is complete.

* Secondary cross-references appear in roman type within the *italicized photo captions*, and alert the curious reader to entries of interest. As with the primary cross-references, these may be used to move through the narrative in a nonsequential fashion; certain bold readers may even wish to traverse the book at random.

The photographs that adorn the volume are the work of a number of artists, whose names and accomplishments are charted in the end matter. These illustrations will doubtless aid the understanding of those seeking to fathom the North American Family.

N O

supposed Straits
of Anian.

A M E

Seal River

Button's Bay

Churchill R

R

New

South Wales

I C A

A FIELD GUIDE TO THE NORTH AMERICAN FAMILY

ADOLESCENCE

It's the boltcutters that open up a hole in the storm fence just big enough for a skinny boy to slip through. It's the backpack in which spraycans are rattling. One knows what one is doing, weaving back and forth among the dark hulks of traincars; it's the rails one must be careful to avoid. It's the memory of batteries blown up in earlier, smaller instances of life beyond the law. Or beyond the row of junked cars, the newer ones the mayor has pronounced paint-resistant. It's the rush of blood in the ears. The image on the backs of the eyes. It's the sky over the city sprayed violet, like the inside of one's heart—cloudy, brooding, still aglow after distant explosions.

01   *Though often identified with* Freedom, *the wild* Adolescence *more closely resembles a Search for* Meaning.

SEE ALSO:
(006) ANGST   (008) BOREDOM   (010) CHEMISTRY
(036) GRAVITY   (082) NATURE VS. NURTURE   (096) REBELLION
(116) TENDERNESS   (124) WHATEVER

ADULTHOOD

Funerals weren't so different from elementary school. There were rules you learned sooner or later, the easy way or the hard way. Sit still. Listen. Offer your wife or daughter a hand to hold, as though holding hands were something your family still did. Squeeze to signify you might cry at what seem to be the appropriate moments. If you think you might actually cry, wear sunglasses. It was grim but true: like school and work and everything else in Jack Hungate's life, the funeral had eventually lost its novelty and become just another thing to plug into the day-planner, and by the end of his forties, he was averaging one or two every year: coworkers, fraternity brothers, relatives he'd forgotten he had. Neighbors. The sun was shining on the day they committed Frank Harrison to the earth, for example, and as Jack gazed through tinted lenses at the glowing blond hair on his own wife's and daughter's heads and at his son's nascent sideburns, he realized he'd never really known the man, despite having seen him at least once a week for the last decade—a total of hundreds of neighborly interactions. Several times each summer, Frank had brought his family over to barbecue and swim. Their kids were the same age, roughly. A memory floated up out of the haze: Frank Harrison emerging from the backyard pool, half-naked and hulking, his booming voice advertising his kingdom for a towel and a beer. And it dawned on Jack that it could just as easily have been his own blood vessels bursting. It could have been *his* heart. He struggled to remain somber. He looked out across the sea of stricken faces toward the faraway silver Sound. Incense was on the air. An eerie silence obtained, as after snowfall, broken only by the priest's litany and the drone of incoming planes and the widow's choked breathing. *It could have been me,* Jack thought, but it wasn't. A month later, when he and Elizabeth separated, he would find himself cursing the empty decorum of the country club set. But it served him well that day; no one could tell that inside he was rejoicing. Or that, although his heart now went out to Marnie and the two Harrison kids, Lacey and whatshisname—Tommy—he'd never really cared for the dead man anyway.

02   Adulthood *can be distinguished from* Maturity *by its tendency to cling to the chrysalis. On occasion,* Adulthood *has even been known to disappear back into* Adolescence *following an unsettling foray into the world.*

ANGST

Gabriel Hungate began to experiment at age thirteen, without the knowledge of his father or mother or younger sister. Described variously as "headstrong," "hard to peg," and "persuasive," he had long been an object of interest among the neighborhood males two to three years his senior. When in a local backyard one offered him a modified aluminum can and the remnants of a "dime bag," he accepted immediately. It might just as easily have started with a Mini-Thin or a dose of Ritalin or a drink of tequila; in the blurred tumble of months that followed Gabriel speculated that, contrary to the rigid verticality of the "gateway hypothesis," stimulants and sedatives were networked horizontally, each linked to every other. Alcohol, nicotine, and cannabis, because the most readily available, were the intoxicants most often used among his cohort and by the subject himself. Typical symptoms of substance abuse (sullenness, academic underachievement, social withdrawal) were masked in Gabriel by a simultaneous disturbance in his domestic situation. His appetite for "downers" was well within the statistical mean for his sex and age; his tendencies to ingest in solitude and to keep the frequency and intensity of his intoxication secret even from his peers were outliers. Gabriel tended to conduct his experiments in his bedroom or the basement recreation room, and to further gauge his limits by playing music at high volume and sitting for hours in the dark in a state of self-recrimination. Even in the "kegger" setting, he drifted toward seclusion, where, he believed, anyone who cared to find him would come looking. No one came looking. Also notable, given the pattern of abuse over several years, was the abrupt cessation of these behaviors. Following the construction of a "graffiti wall" in the backyard of his mother's house, Gabriel Hungate, for reasons beyond the explanatory power of this study, gave up narcotics at an age (17) when most of his peers were intensifying their explorations. He began, instead, to paint (although, significantly, the patterns of withdrawal and self-reproach and heavy tobacco use would continue right up until his accident).

03 *The fossil record shows the juvenile strain of* Angst *to be a relative newcomer. Possibly the product of crossbreeding between* Boredom *and* Depression, *it made its first documented appearance fewer than five hundred years ago.*

BOREDOM

Jackie roams the near-empty lower field with a handheld video camera, chasing the electrons in the broody gray air, the mist so fine it might be imaginary. Brakelights stream beyond the chainlink fence. On the next field over, the varsity football team is practicing, and the war chants of teenagers puncture the pressurized quiet. A flock of graywhite birds is flushed from the hedge that separates the two fields. She chases them, her ponytail whipping around, her skirt and shirt too thin for the weather. She is narrating. "Today I lost a tooth." She captures the birds as they tumble in a dizzying fractal into the air, colors shifting light to dark. They churn over a swimming pool that's been covered for winter and dwindle to dots in the sky. "They're running away. They don't like me," Jackie says. Trees scatter in the lens as she gallops away from the bushes. "The grass is brown." She spots a mudpuddle. "This is from when the trucks come across the field for a delivery." Now she lies down in the dry grass and aims the camera toward her face. "This is what it's like to be a bug. Not very exciting." She turns the camera around and positions her stuffed lion in front of the lens. It flops over. She reaches out to make an adjustment, but it flops again. An empty sandbox forms a backdrop. "This is Alphonse," she says. "Say hello, Alphonse. Hello! Behind him, that's the sandbox where I played at lunch today. I made a castle. Tomorrow I'm going to play kickball. That's my video journal for today. The end." The microphone drones dimly with white noise, and the camera continues to run, capturing the sandbox and the procession of blurry taillights far behind the flopped lion, whose mane is accreting fine raindrops. The voice cuts in again. "Oh, and also today, my parents got divorced. The end." The footage ends abruptly.

04

Once thought to be nonexistent where there was Entertainment, *this harmless parasite is now known to abide, to some degree, in every ecosystem.*

CHEMISTRY

Sugar. Sweet & Low. Caffeine to start the day. To unwind, alcohol: a beer or
two, a glass of wine. Sherry or gin or a dry martini, by the chair by the pool,
a glass or a bottle. Then Tylenol. Or, for headaches, ibuprofen. For asthma,
albuterol. Sniffles, sneezes, post-nasal drip: Robitussin, Nyquil, Dimetapp.
The pantheon of name-brand pharmaceuticals, like poets of a dead tongue:
Valium, Lithium, Xanax and Zoloft, Paxil and Prozac. Allegra, Viagra. Claritin,
Clarinex, Retsin and Ritalin. The shelf in the medicine chest stuffed with Eli
Lilly, GlaxoSmithKline, AstraZeneca. The horizons huffing opens up: gasoline,
whipped cream, permanent markers, airplane glue, and airbrush propellant.
And then nicotine. Marijuana. Hashish. Opium. Amyl nitrates. Lysergic acid
diethylamide. Psilocybin. Mescaline. Methamphetamines and amphetamines.
Cocaine to kill pain. No different than a codeine pill. No different than Demerol,
or Percocet. The baby aspirin doctors recommend most. The epidural, even
before the birth.

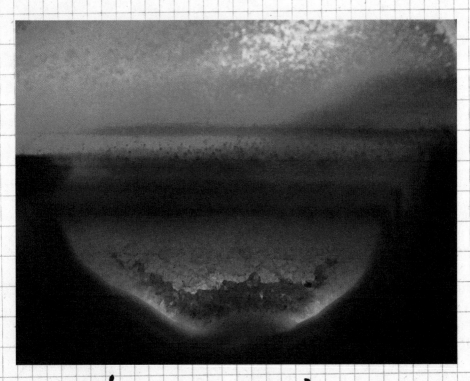

05   Chemistry *is an order of the phylum* Entertainment.

SEE ALSO:
(004) ADULTHOOD   (006) ANGST   (008) BOREDOM
(018) DEPRESSION   (042) HABITS, BAD   (072) MEAN... ...EARCH F...
(076) MOMENT OF CLARITY   (086) PARTINGS   (1.. ...SECRET
(120) UNCERTAINTY

COMMITMENT

At first the black lady behind the desk said visiting hours were over. I could understand where she was coming from—she could have lost her job for breaking hospital regulations—so I tried to keep smiling, because I didn't want her to feel bad about what was, after all, just doing her job. But like my dad used to say back when he was still alive, I have a lousy poker face, and after a few seconds, she sighed. "All right. Tell me what's going on." Her face was businesslike, but her eyes were kind, I noticed. And it just started spilling out of me, about cheerleading running over and Tommy being late with the car and how it would be so hard for me to get across town to the hospital by eight on Tuesdays and Thursdays to see my boyfriend, the patient. She asked his name and I told her, Hungate. Gabriel. She found his chart and studied it for a minute. "Like the archangel," she said, pronouncing the *h*. Then she told me that she was in charge on weeknights and, so long as I didn't tell anyone, she'd take me back to see him whenever I could get here. That's how I started going every night to the burn unit. It was kind of nice, actually, after all the visitors were gone, even his family, and it could be just him and me. I could talk to him and read to him and sometimes just sit quietly with my hand resting on his one unbandaged hand and try to feel him talking to me through his skin. I could cry and nobody would know. That's another thing my dad had told me: I led a charmed life, everything would always work out for me. His voice was staticky when he said it; we must have had a bad connection. And on Christmas Eve morning I made sugar cookies from scratch. It started snowing as I drove over to the hospital to leave them at the front desk for the nurse who'd bent the rules for me. It turned out she was on vacation. Still, I left them for whoever was scheduled to work that night.

06   *Though sightings are rare, this ancestor of* Fidelity *can be observed in the wild to this day.*

SEE ALSO:
(036) GRAVITY   (058) INTEGRITY   (090) PRIVACY
(116) TENDERNESS

CONSENSUS

We can all agree on this much, Marnie thought: nobody saw the Hungate divorce coming. Of course she'd heard through her daughter that Jack and Elizabeth had been having some difficulties, but what couple didn't? Lord knows Frank had sometimes gone for months without touching her and had sometimes worked late and had sometimes retreated to his study with his *Wall Street Journal* without so much as asking about anyone else's day. But at those times, Marnie had looked to the Hungates. In the privacy of her own mind, she saw them as the last of a dying breed, the Great American Family. She'd actually found herself wondering: WWED? What Would Elizabeth Do? Other times, she even felt a little jealous of her slender, blond neighbor with her sensitive husband and her popular son and her still-small daughter and her big, kidney-shaped swimming pool. It was by that swimming pool, in fact, on the first warm day after Frank died, that Marnie found herself eyeing a paring knife as Elizabeth lounged nearby in a two-piece, not really listening to the answers to her questions. But Marnie'd had years of experience smiling and swallowing, and she reminded herself that some people had all the luck. It wasn't anyone's fault, that's just the way it was. So she was shocked when Lacey announced at breakfast a few weeks later that Gabe's parents were separating. No one at the Friends of the Library cookout could agree on what caused it. Some people insinuated Jack Hungate was having an affair, but personally, Marnie didn't buy it. Jack had always been a stand-up guy, and she didn't approve of scuttlebutt. Nonetheless, she found herself wanting to know more about the divorce, and every time the subject came up she felt a little flutter of something like gratitude, for which on Sundays she always confessed.

07   *The life of a* Consensus *is fleeting; in a single day it hatches, finds a mate, gives birth, and dies.*

CUSTODY BATTLE

When your house is never clean enough. When your food is never healthy enough. When you're perpetually five to fifteen minutes late to meet them in the parking lot of Ken's Big Boy, the neutral zone where your estranged wife insists you meet to exchange your daughter on Wednesdays and alternating weekends. Her Volvo, formerly yours, will be waiting, the sun on the windshield obscuring the passengers within. She always leaves the engine running these days, as if to underscore the point: you're not on time, and she has places to be. Your daughter will adopt these grievances as her own, but they will retain the familiar tang of Elizabeth, like the pillowcase that still smells of her shampoo. Like the photos in the yearbooks you left behind when you moved out.

08   *Descended from* Divorce, Custody Battle *is one of several natural predators of the Amicable* Parting.

SEE ALSO:

(038) GRIEF   (054) INFIDELITY   (088) PHASE

(100) RECONCILIATION   (106) SACRIFICE   (118) TRADITION

DEPRESSION

Instant oatmeal for breakfast. It was always instant oatmeal in the winter.
I had grown bored with the available flavors: Maple & Brown Sugar, Apples &
Cinnamon, Raisins & Spice. Once, there had been a Cinnamon & Spice, but now
you had to make your own by excavating all the raisins, moving them to one side of
the bowl. I used the convex part of the spoon to smooth out little trenches in the
surface of the oatmeal and then watched as they filled up with milk. "You're not
hungry, Tommy?" my mom wanted to know. She was packing lunches on the other
side of the kitchen island. I told her my stomach hurt, which was partially true, in
that it would hurt by the time I got to school if I didn't eat something. "You look
tired," she said. The milk wasn't filling the trenches fast enough. I hacked out deep
crevasses with the end of the spoon. I rolled the raisins in and covered them over.
I told her I had been up late doing homework. Really, I had been lying under the
covers naked and stoned, listening to the noises that meant my sister and Gabe
were dry-humping instead of studying in the next room, or rather the lack of noise,
the silence that seeped through the Sheetrock and the pillow. Wondering if Gabe
had felt this way back when he was using. Sometimes at school I said things that
maybe were a little exaggerated to appear more interesting, but I usually tried to
be honest with my mom. It was just that with my dad gone, there were certain
things I couldn't tell her. I couldn't tell her, for example, that half the kids last year
had thought I was making it up about Dad until Lacey confirmed the reason we'd
been absent for a week. I couldn't tell her that I couldn't sleep anymore unless I
masturbated beforehand. And I couldn't tell her that this fucking breakfast made
me want to puke. I pretended to take a couple bites and then, when her back was
turned, got up and dumped the bowl down the garbage disposal. I pulled on my
backpack full of stolen compact discs and graphing calculators and pecked her on
the cheek and breezed out the front door, trying to give the impression that, on this
day like every other, there was anything to look forward to.

09 *Evolved from a ruminant species known as Melancholia,* Depression *now dominates the animal kingdom. Its rapid expansion remains unaccounted for, but some Family-watchers have pointed to a concurrent surge in Search for* Meaning.

SEE ALSO:
(002) ADOLESCENCE   (004) ADULTHOOD

DISCRETION

She would never say who, and there were times when Jack wondered whether knowing his identity would have made it better or worse—afternoons that first fall when he sat on the back porch with a Schaefer and a cigarette, ready to hide the latter at the first hint of a car pulling into the drive. False alarms were constant. He would stub out the butt halfway through, only to gather from the unbroken silence of the house behind him that the engine whine he'd heard heralded the arrival of one of his new neighbors, and not his son. He'd given Gabe a little used Geo for his seventeenth birthday back in September, when he and Elizabeth were still wavering about the separation, like the two last leaves on a branch (as though there were anything to do but give in to gravity). Now he wondered if this wasn't part of what kept Gabe coming back, some obscure sense of obligation. Certainly Jackie had added the car to an already formidable dossier of evidence that her father favored his firstborn. The scent of tobacco that hovered around Gabe when he appeared in the afternoons after school made Jack pretty sure that his son was secretly a smoker, too. But what could he say? Besides, it almost made him feel closer to the boy. And perhaps Gabe made the crosstown trip so often (far more than the custody agreement stipulated) just to have an excuse to be in the car alone, where he could smoke in private. Jackie never visited anymore. In this way and in most others, she and her brother offset each other. Jack scanned the new backyard. Maybe he would build a wall here that Gabe could paint on, as Elizabeth had reportedly done. The sky, hemmed in by the evergreens at the edges of the backyard, was gray, and had been for weeks. The grass was getting crispy. The wind that gusted up and rattled the wind chimes was nothing like it used to be, off the bay. At the old house, he couldn't have gotten the cigarette lit. He decided he would have felt better knowing if it had been Martin Luther King and worse if it had been Jack Kennedy. Better if it was Eric Clapton and worse if it was Peter Frampton. Better knowing if it was over. Worse if it was still going on. Better knowing if it was a complete stranger. Otherwise, better to remain in the dark.

10

N.B.: Discretion *and* Privacy *are not the same animal.*

SEE ALSO:
(004) ADULTHOOD   (042) HABITS, BAD   (058) INTEGRITY
(094) QUESTIONS, NAGGING   (102) RESIGNATION   (104) RUMOR
(108) SECRET

DIVORCE

He knew, oh, he knew, he saw it coming, he kept asking her, while she gardened, while she unloaded the dishwasher, while she flipped again through the takeout menus unable to find what she wanted, are you happy, Mom, are you happy, knowing somehow she wasn't, and no, the knowing didn't make it any better, because another thing he knew, like he knew his own face in the mirror, was that it was his fault, because what was Mom doing, sitting in the corner of the living room with the headphones on every night that week, if not taking a cue from her son . . . if not, herself, withdrawing? He heard folk music sloshing out of the headphones like water over the rim of a bowl. He had half a mind to go through Mom's underwear drawer, to see if she, too, had a stash. Then Dad, on the couch with an accordion file, was asking her a question that she, in her headphones, couldn't hear, and asking again, louder. And then both voices were raised, as Gabe had known they would be—something had happened, as he had known it would— and he went to the basement with the lights off and took the last two pills from the film canister in his pocket and swallowed them without water and knelt in the middle of the rug, and he swore it would be the last time, but oh, he knew, he had done it, he had done it now.

11   *Due to a growth curve similar to that of* Depression, *a robust* Divorce
population has become common wherever Love *dwells in large numbers.*

ENTERTAINMENT

In the beginning was the Television. And the Television was large and paneled in plastic made to look like wood. It dwelled in a dim corner of the living room and came on for national news, *Cosby*, Saturday cartoons, and football. And man and woman huddled close on the sofa or stretched out on the rug, and it was good. When man made partner, they bought a VCR, and soon afterward another Television, and they began to watch videos together in the darkness. And there was popcorn. In the fifth year, the cable company created the premium-channel package. And it was affordable. And woman had moved up in the mayor's office, and so they said why not. After days of toil, to sit and feast in front of the Television and not to have to think of something to say was for man and woman a kind of heaven. And then Nintendo said: Let there be Duck Hunt. Let there be Mario Brothers. Let there be Nintendo 64 and GameCube. And the children saw that these were good, though to watch and play at once was not possible. Thus was there purchased a children's Television, and unto it was given its own room. And thus did the furnished basement come to be a refuge for daughter and son when the silence upstairs ended and the fighting began. Where once they had sat together squabbling over the controllers, they now took turns occupying the room alone, turning up the sound to drown out the voices through the floorboards. And save for the screen's blue light, darkness was on the faces of the children.

12 *With its rapid mutation rate,* Entertainment *adapts readily to changes in the environment. Easily housebroken, it is welcomed in most North American* Homes.

FAMILY VALUES

Long after his life ceased to resemble the one he'd imagined for himself as a kid—after pressed slacks replaced bluejeans, a house on Long Island replaced the East Side walkup, the rush of a massive short position replaced that of a line of blow, and he ceased to recognize the Brooklyn girl he couldn't keep his hands off in the overweight homemaker he'd married—Frank listened to the Who. He kept disc three of the boxed set in the Suburban at all times and disc four in his Discman. The world around him no longer struck power chords, but stranded in rush-hour traffic or lifting weights at his overpriced gym, he could still feel locked inside his ribs the hunger that had found its perfect expression in "The Seeker," in "Won't Get Fooled Again." Even when there was no music, the Who played in his head. It was "Who Are You" that he was hearing this afternoon, in the Hungates' backyard. He was standing with Jack by the grill, ostensibly absorbing the details of some legal case, but all that was in his head was "Who are you? Who, who, who, who?" He lit another cigarette and looked over at the pool. Tommy was standing in the shallow end, a wet white tee-shirt clinging to his flabby boy-breasts. He was sticking his tongue out at the little Hungate girl, Jackie, who was sticking her tongue out at him. Tommy's tongue disappeared when Elizabeth knelt at the edge of the water to ask him if he wanted a Coke. She wore a tee-shirt over her bikini top; her tanned legs folded under her. Frank felt a stirring beneath his swim trunks . . . and then embarrassment as the boy said, "Yeah." "How about a thank-you?" Frank called to him. "That's my boy," he added, after his flushed son had stammered out his gratitude; he didn't want her to think that they weren't close, he and Tommy, or that he wasn't the kind and caring father he in point of fact was. And before rising to disappear into the house, she rewarded him with a brief smile. He apologized to Jack. "We just really emphasize respect in our house. You were saying?" Out of guilt for his impure thoughts, he worked extra-hard to give the illusion that he was listening, but the Roger Daltrey in his head kept screaming, "Who the fuck are you?"

13   *Specimens of this type—a toy breed of* Tradition—*are recognizable by their seeming delicacy and attractive plumage. Be careful handling* Family Values, *however: beneath the surface lies a savage carnality.*

SEE ALSO:
(018) DEPRESSION   (020) DISCRETION   (030) FISCAL RESPONSIBILITY
(040) GUILT   (072) MEANING, SEARCH FOR   (074) MIDLIFE CRISIS
(078) MORTGAGE   (120) UNCERTAINTY

FIDELITY

Like that time? The time we totally knew but were afraid to tell you that that boyfriend of yours was messing around with your former supposed friend Michelle, who we can now all agree is a total bitch and who sometimes we secretly think would have been a match made in heaven for Gabe in terms of being way selfish and also spacey if what happened hadn't happened, and he was probably like tattooing swans on her forearms with a ballpoint or something the way he did to win you over? That whole time if you would have just brought your concerns to us we would have known you wouldn't be totally shattered to learn the truth. Because, I mean, we were always looking out for you, girl, that's what you do when you care. When he got third-degree burns over eighty percent of his body, for example. Because after that that skank washed her hands of him, but you, you were able to forgive, maybe because there was more to him than we knew but probably more because you're pretty much incapable of cruelty.

14   Fidelity *is a lesser-known relative of the more common* Infidelity.

SEE ALSO:
(012) COMMITMENT   (022) DIVORCE   (036) GRAVITY
(044) HABITS, GOOD   (058) INTEGRITY   (082) NATURE VS. NURTURE
(090) PRIVACY   (108) SECRET

FISCAL RESPONSIBILITY

Not to put too fine a point on it, Mr. and Ms. Big-Time GOPAC contributor, but the private sector ain't going to offer to pick up the tab when, after a gruesome accident and a three-month hospital stay, your son's medical bills pass the million-dollar mark. Although, on second thought, it will employ the doctor who'll wield the scalpel during the skin grafts, so maybe it's all right after all. And think of all the magazines you'll read in the waiting room! The sweet efflorescence of the media conglomerates! Think of the market-driven advances in chair design! The commercials on the television in the corner! Now, all in all, aren't you feeling pretty good about the private sector?

15   *Though often identified with* Freedom, *this household pest typically exists in symbiosis with* Mortgage. *It can be found wherever there is sufficient* Material.

SEE ALSO:

(010) CHEMISTRY   (048) HIERARCHY   (102) RESIGNATION

FREEDOM

Elizabeth's been working out. Kicking along with her tae bo video. Listening to mid-period Joni Mitchell while she runs in front of the big picture window on a treadmill rescued from the obscurity of the garage. Reading Susan Faludi and Anaïs Nin. Country line-dancing and wearing tall boots and eating ice cream for lunch. She's been doing things she never would have when she was married to Jack. She's been doing things because she never would have when she was married to Jack. She's constantly aware of all that's broken or lost: the trust of her son, the happiness of her daughter, the comforting warm lump of a husband in the bed beside her, the narrative thrust of her life, but she's been telling herself it was worth it. And on a country road on the North Fork one day, edging the Volvo's speedometer over 90 miles per hour, just because she can, she wonders, does this count as liberation?

16   *Perhaps because of its resemblance to the endangered* Meaning, Freedom *is the single most sought-after creature in North America. Like* Entertainment, *it is increasingly valued as a delicacy in other parts of the world.*

SEE ALSO:
(002) ADOLESCENCE   (012) COMMITMENT   (022) DIVORCE
(056) INNOCENCE   (074) MIDLIFE CRISIS   (084) OPTIMISM
(096) REBELLION   (122) VULNERABILITY

FRIEND OF THE FAMILY

Neither boy can remember a time when he has not known the other; their houses are separated only by two long sections of chain-link fence and a high-strung schnauzer bitch named Tiffany who patrols the Perlmutters' backyard, directing her piercing bark at any person or animal who comes within fifty yards. The two families have been close since their mothers discovered they were both due in September of 1986, one with the boy who would be Gabriel and the other with the girl she would name Lacey. Marnie and Elizabeth still swim and talk; Frank and Jack swap lawn equipment; Lacey plays surrogate mother to Jackie. It is strange, then, that the boys, only fourteen months apart, have never really been friendly. Gabriel, when given the choice, has always gravitated toward the older kids in the neighborhood, who spurn roly-poly little Tommy Harrison. Gabe himself has never really trusted Tommy, with his incessant blinking and puppydog obsequiousness and outrageous brags. And, since the time Gabe told the other kids about the younger boy's demonstrably false claim to have a bowling alley in his basement— that is, since the nickname "Lying Tommy" made its way back to the bearer— he's been uncomfortably sure the feeling must be mutual.

17 Friend *or* Friends *was once common in almost every North American Family. Competition from* Entertainment *appears to have thinned its numbers substantially.*

SEE ALSO:
(006) ANGST   (048) HIERARCHY   (072) MEANING, SEARCH FOR
(082) NATURE VS. NURTURE   (092) PROVIDENCE   (098) RECOGNITION
(124) WHATEVER

GRAVITY

The garage is where it first happened. He was supposed to clean it out for like ten dollars or something. My mom had sent me over to borrow an edge-trimmer, and Mrs. Hungate told me to go into the garage and ask him to help me find it. At first I couldn't see him. It was dim in there with the single bulb and all. Even though it was the kind of garage with windows, it was a gray day outside at the end of August. I remember there was a tennis ball strung from the ceiling like a Hangman. Kind of creepy. Then I heard this clackety-clack sound from the other side of the car. I walked around the rear bumper and saw him squatting there on the concrete pad, arranging aerosol cans in a milk crate. He jumped a little at the sound of his name. He was like, Do you want something? and I told him about the edge-trimmer. He softened after that; I guess I had just scared him. We were seventeen and hadn't talked in forever, since the time I pushed him into the pool for trying to give me a wedgie. Or at least in the year since my dad had died. Gabe was a foot taller than he'd been back when I had had my crush on him, and something else . . . more secretive, I guess. Quieter. He got the edge-trimmer out from wherever it was and put it in my hand and said, "Anything else?" I think it was raining outside. I told him I was sorry about his parents. He stared at me like he might slap me. "I'd rather not talk about it," he said. I told him I had been there. Boy, had I. But when I apologized, he said "Don't be sorry." Next thing I'm sitting on the hood of his mom's Volvo with his waist in between my knees and we're kissing. I had kissed boys before, but not like that. Not like fighting and kissing at the same time, with our belt buckles scraping together. When I said I'd better go, what I meant was Tell me to stay, but he didn't. I spent a couple weeks in agony before he called me on the phone and said, "So what are you doing?"

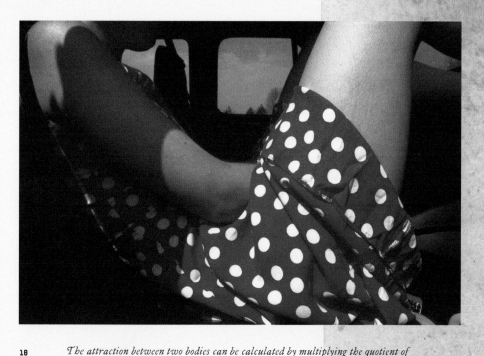

18 *The attraction between two bodies can be calculated by multiplying the quotient of the product of their combined mass and the square of the distance between them by the universal gravitational constant, G.*

SEE ALSO:
(002) ADOLESCENCE   (018) DEPRESSION   (028) FIDELITY
(060) INTIMACY   (076) MOMENT OF CLARITY   (104) RUMOR
(116) TENDERNESS   (120) UNCERTAINTY

GRIEF

Less than a month after Gabe's accident she was back in the gym in her pep squad whites, her feet falling into the complicated floor-work as though she'd been gone only a weekend. If she'd lost anything, it was just the inside track for next year's head cheerleader position, the goodwill that would have accrued from four more weeks of closeness with the other girls. She would never have imagined, or desired, that the sympathy they now felt toward her had virtually guaranteed her the spot. That her best friend and closest competitor, Michelle DuPlessis, was ready to step aside for her. Lacey didn't let the subject come up, didn't give Michelle an opening. Instead, she hurled herself brightly into the new routines, clapping, slapping her hips, shaking her ass, springing into the air, dropping to the parquet, spiraling back up, her pointer finger thrust into the air, her exultant smile so well-rehearsed as to seem completely spontaneous. She sweated a little more than usual—she was out of shape and this was strenuous work—but she resisted the urge to put her hands on her thighs during breaks. At the end of practice, when it was time to make the pyramid, the girls insisted that she reclaim her place at the top. She was, after all, the lightest. As she rose, lofted by the soft hands on her legs and back, she forgot, for a moment, that she'd ever been gone at all. From the top of the pyramid, it was hard to imagine that anyone died ever. And if later she slumped a little bit on the locker-room bench, waiting for the other girls to finish showering before she took off her clothes, no one was so gauche as to let her know they noticed.

19   *Slow to adapt to ecological upheaval,* Grief *now thrives only in isolation.*
      Its study is further complicated by its nocturnal Habits, *and by the fact that*
      no Grief *is like any other.*

SEE ALSO:
(012) COMMITMENT   (018) DEPRESSION   (022) DIVORCE
(030) FISCAL RESPONSIBILITY   (032) FREEDOM
(072) MEANING, SEARCH FOR   (074) MIDLIFE CRISIS
(102) RESIGNATION

GUILT

"Oh, you know . . . Since pretty much as far back as I can remember." And how far back can you remember? "Everything's a question with you guys, isn't it?" Does that make you uncomfortable? "No, no. It's just . . ." He laughs, not wholly convincingly. "Okay, you want a story, I'll give you a story. We were all on a school trip to the roller-skating rink. Galaxy of Sports, it was called. Gabe and Lacey were in second grade or something, I must have been in first, maybe even kindergarten. There was this girl I was crazy about, with the hair bow and the curls that were begging to be pulled. Jenny. Jenny Lehotsky. Why are you looking at me like that?" I'm not looking at you like anything, Thomas. Keep going. "Well, I thought maybe Jenny and I could go roller-skating, maybe hold hands. I mean Gabe and my sister were probably already doing Olympic routines at the center of the rink, but this girl was scared or something. She spent, I don't know . . . an hour hanging around the snack bar. And then she took some money out of her pocket and proceeded to clean them out. They sold these candy sticks, these barbershop spirals, lemon swirled with lime, butterscotch swirled with cream, and when she turned around with a huge handful I swear it was the most beautiful thing I'd ever seen. She starts handing the candy sticks out to her friends, friends who unwrap them and eat them incredibly slowly, making those noises of enjoyment. Yum. Slurp. Mmm. My dad, of course, has taken the position that he's already shelling out five bucks for the damn skate rental, and no I may not have any money for snacks. So naturally I ask my beloved, you know, you've got like fifty of those, could I have one? Nope, she says. And I watch her put the rest of them in the locker where her shoes are. Well, what am I supposed to do, when she goes off to skate with her friends and leaves the locker unlocked? Guilty, your honor. I stole a butterscotch candy stick and hid behind the Whac-A-Mole machine to eat it. But here's the interesting part: I couldn't. I took one bite, and immediately I saw my dad's face, my dad kneeling at the communion rail, that why-me-lord look he got, and the candy just turned to ash in my mouth. I went and turned myself in to the teacher and asked to be punished. She probably thought it was hilarious, this little kid looking for absolution for stealing like two cents' worth of candy that probably should have been given to him anyway. But she bit her tongue and told me to go tell my victim what I'd done. Which is the last time I ever stole anything. Not to mention the last time Michelle ever talked to me." Jenny? "Right. Jenny."

20 *Onlookers generally agree that* Guilt *is essential to the healthy ecosystem, though recent genomic variation has led to some weakening in parent-offspring transmission.*

SEE ALSO:
(026) FAMILY VALUES   (048) HIERARCHY   (066) MATERIAL
(070) MATURITY   (072) MEANING, SEARCH FOR
(098) RECOGNITION   (114) TANTRUM

HABITS, BAD

You'll see them first thing in the morning, like dew on the lawns, and last thing at night, in the gaps where the motion sensors won't detect them. They believe they're invisible like this, in the shadows, but if you study the postures of the figures hunched on front stoops and in bathroom windows by box fans and slumped in lawn chairs out back, you will recognize congressmen, judges, PTA chairs, pillars of the community, sometimes even your own parents or children— the secret smokers. Each cigarette is a stitch binding their lives more tightly together: the cigarettes Jack sneaks behind the modest bungalow literally on the other side of the tracks from the old place on the water; the cigarettes that drove Frank's blood pressure up by imperceptible degrees; the cigarettes Gabe chain-smokes on his long nocturnal drives to wherever it is he disappears to; the ones Lacey smells on his breath that make her want to ask him to choose, her or Philip Morris, even as she leans in for another kiss.

Depending on parent genotype, the crossbreeding of a Bad Habit *and* Boredom *will result in either* Chemistry *or* Entertainment.

SEE ALSO:
(044) HABITS, GOOD

HABITS, GOOD

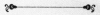

There is no such thing as a good habit.

For identification of all habits, see Habits, Bad.

HEIRLOOM

It wasn't like I planned it, exactly. Sometimes in the summer it was just, you know, drive out to where the tracks end at night, see what comes your way. Out there, the parking lots went on for acres. You could smoke a tree and watch the sky, the planes streaking in to Islip, if you were feeling that certain way. Or you might ride out there with some of your boys and just fuck with people. I never really got in anybody's face like that before, but I guess a gun's got a mind of its own. Like in *Lord of the Rings,* like it's using you to complete its destiny. Or I don't know, maybe I was just fucked up. The gun was my uncle's who went upstate—I borrowed it off my cousin after I got hassled by some Spanish dudes. Protection and whatnot. I didn't really plan to use it, just keep it to show, if necessary. And then I'm sitting out there all red-eyed on the trunk of my man's car in a parking lot in Suffolk County, and he nudges me like, see that? And I look across all those empty puddles of light at this tall, ghost-looking shadow coming toward us. "You see that? He just gave you the finger, son." I knew it wasn't true, but the kid was walking like he owned the island and didn't have to think about nothing. I'm like, I'll give him something to think about. I walked up alongside him and asked for a dollar, like for a Coke. He just kept on walking, paint all on his pants like some kind of art-school fag. I'm like, "You hear me?" And he just says, "I hear you." But looking somewhere to the left of my head all spacey. So that's when I go, hear this, then, motherfucker. It felt good in my hand, the waffled grip, like all the years of Duck Hunt and then Bond had been preparing me. He was probably my age. It was like some movie I can't remember the name of: the two of us, same height, same build, moving through our different lives to this one moment where we tested each other all the way down. And the thing is, he won. Because of the look in his eyes, that look in them like, just go on ahead and shoot me. That made it real. I'm like, "Fuck this" and ran to the car and we mashed out. Later, I tried to lie, say I got his wallet, but my man asked to see it. All I had to show was eight bucks and a bus transfer, which I'd had when we rode out there.

23 *The reappearance of the* Heirloom, *which happens only once per generation, is not to be missed by connoisseurs of* Meaning.

SEE ALSO:
(006) ANGST   (008) BOREDOM   (010) CHEMISTRY
(048) HIERARCHY   (080) MYTHOLOGY   (082) NATURE VS. NURTURE
(096) REBELLION   (118) TRADITION   (124) WHATEVER

HIERARCHY

There were two kinds of people, Tommy reflected as he walked past the big, detached, Cape Cod–style houses, the porches with their extravagant pumpkins: those who are It and those who are Not-It. Differentiation began at an early age, in backyards and playgrounds. Some Not-Its, through an elaborate and invisible sensory apparatus, were able to intuit the precise instant a game began, and to shout "Not It" to the world. The rest learned fairly quickly to chime in whenever the call of "Not It" arose, and thereby to escape solitude. Not-Its called the games. Not-Its set the rules. Not-Its grew up to own houses of the type Tommy was now passing, spacious and freestanding and painted to look as though they'd always been there, with pumpkins large enough to feed entire Third World villages. It was mid-October, and the streets near school were empty; having skipped sixth period, he was too early for the flood of Not-It kids that would sluice down these sidewalks at three p.m. When the wind stirred, the leaves made a pleasant scudding sound on the concrete. He veered off the sidewalk to kick at a leaf pile. Tommy was surrounded by Not-Its. His dad, for example. And Gabe. The first to shout, the ones with the best toys. His sister and Mrs. Hungate fell in effortlessly. But Tommy, through some quirk of genetics, had always been an It. Every group needed one. The one whose voice lingered alone and false when all the others had faded from the air: "Not It!" The one who stayed behind when the Not-Its ran away. He swerved again to kick at another pile of leaves, doubtless raked by day laborers imported from Plainview and Hicksville and Queens to keep the yards tidy. He was hoping to uncover a mulchy underworld of worms and wriggling, but wouldn't you know it? It hadn't rained for weeks.

24

Believed by ancient cultures to ward off Anarchy *and* Misfortune
(cf. CLAN, COURT AND CLOISTER: A POCKET ALMANAC),
Hierarchy *is now seen as vulnerable to attack from many of the great*
predators that stalk the Family.

SEE ALSO:
(004) ADULTHOOD   (012) COMMITMENT   (018) DEPRESSION   (040) GUILT
(072) MEANING, SEARCH FOR   (120) UNCERTAINTY

HOLIDAY

Nowadays we split them all, right down the middle of the day, so that the kids might, for example, be with Jack until noon on Christmas, and then with me for the standing rib roast and the evening afterward. Soon Gabe will be off at college, and then Jackie, and it hardly seems worth getting a big tree anymore. That was always Jack's thing anyway. We're paying for the high ceilings, was his reasoning, why not use them? Every year he and Gabe would come back from their expedition with a tree bigger than the last. It would take the three of us just to get it through the door. Still, I have to admit, with all the lights and all of the million Christmas ornaments Jack's mother had given to us from her private hoard, it looked beautiful. Some nights when the kids had gone to bed he and I would lie back on the sofa and just watch it. I remember the way the big back window doubled the lights, a multicolored galaxy in a slick black sky. Our tenth Christmas Eve after we moved out of the city, back when the tree was modest, we were lying like that taking a breather before putting the presents out. Gazing at the tree, at the glitter-strewn star we'd just placed on top, I still felt fat from the pregnancy, but it didn't seem to matter to Jack. His hands had begun to explore the skin between navel and elastic when Gabe appeared on the stairs crying. He must have been nine. Jackie had just started sleeping through the night. I asked him what was wrong, expecting him to say that he'd had a bad dream, that he needed the light on. Instead he managed to explain, in fits and starts, that he'd been thinking about all the toys we'd given him that he'd abandoned after playing with for a week or two. He'd been thinking about how lonely they were, sitting at the top of the closet, and how disappointed we must be, and how there were kids in Africa who didn't have any toys. I told him it was okay, we would donate the old toys to some kids right here on Long Island who might like them. I barely managed to keep a straight face as I told him to go back to bed, Santa would be here soon. And then as soon as he was gone I found myself crying, too. He was a funny kid like that.

25   *The* Holiday *may be observed as many as eight times a year. A peaceable
creature, it abhors confrontation; all conflicts within the pack are settled via
high-frequency communications inaudible to the human ear.*

SEE ALSO:
(012) COMMITMENT   (016) CUSTODY BATTLE
(030) FISCAL RESPONSIBILITY   (068) MATERNAL INSTINCT
(076) MOMENT OF CLARITY   (110) SECURITY   (126) YOUTH

HOME

They came to Long Island in search of sunlight. Not the kind that trickled down like water through the fingers of a skyline, but the kind that spread like butter across a green expanse of lawn. They came to Long Island for the relative quiet, the soothing bugsong in summer, in winter the cold crash of waves. They came for the view of those waves, for the big picture window in the living room that looked out over the pool, the trees, the backyard, the breakwater. They came for the community, the neighborhood, the schools. All it cost was a thirty-year mortgage, club dues and greens fees, and train fare to the city five days a week. There were good years in these houses and in these yards. There were pickup basketball games in the driveways, with the kids. There were parties. There were Halloweens and Thanksgivings. And if, after the switch to standard time, they got home well after dark; and if gradually the kids became strangers; and if when the lights were out they only fell asleep exhausted . . . well, was that so different from what their own parents had done, chasing their own dreams of America?

26

Once highly localized in its Habits, *the* Home *has become increasingly nomadic in the last century. It has been known to travel great distances to secure a source of the* Mortgages *on which it subsists.*

INFIDELITY

Tommy made things up for the therapist, told him what he thought he wanted to hear. I wanted to be just like him, he said. It's my fault, he said. Why? Because if I could have been there in time, I could have dialed 911 and Dad would still be alive. He thought he was being clever. Because what he would never, never, never tell the therapist or anyone else was that there had been times lately when he had secretly wished for something like this to happen. His dad, after all, had been cheating on his mom for half a year—he'd overheard him whispering into the phone, when he thought no one was listening. To Tommy it felt as though, in some obscure way, his dad had been cheating on him. The code had been breached, and would never quite make sense again.

27   Infidelity *is the hollow-boned relative of the lesser-known* Fidelity.

INNOCENCE

Jackie continues to make solid academic progress this term. Her verbal gifts and acute imagination have translated into some distinctive creative writing, although her spelling remains unorthodox, perhaps willfully so. Certainly Jackie is a voracious reader, when allowed to choose her own books from the school library. In our Social Studies unit we are encouraging all of our students to try to see historical events from multiple perspectives. While Math is sometimes a challenge for Jackie, consolidating basic skills will help her tackle more complex problems. Any parental support with homework would, of course, be welcome. But our major goals for the remainder of the year are social in nature. Although Jackie is often gregarious with adults, she tends to alternate between somewhat withdrawn and rather dominant behavior patterns within her peer group. This is typical of a developmental stage earlier than the highly socialized phase many of her classmates have entered. As discussed at her midyear conference, her difficulty forming and sustaining close relationships with other girls may be related to unresolved feelings about her parents' divorce. Her controlled demeanor appears to mask a child of extreme sensitivity. Although we understand Jackie's resistance, and wish to respect her unique spirituality, we continue to recommend that she meet with the school counselor regularly and that she attend our monthly grief lunches. It is the school's belief that learning to adapt to change at a young age will promote health of mind and body throughout the many challenges our students will encounter across the grades to come.

Although the life expectancy of Innocence was once believed to be only a few years, recent findings reveal that Innocence can persist in a state of semi-hibernation decades after its initial burst of activity.

INTEGRITY

What attracts people to each other? The question has puzzled humans throughout the ages. Still we know little, except that the nature of attraction is irrational. Hypothetically speaking, a female professional in her early forties should have little rational incentive to stray from a marriage that has yielded two healthy children. Even were the most virile man to express interest, she would hardly be able to find time for a dalliance amid her busy schedule. Indeed, time is the one thing missing from her marriage (again, hypothetically). Yet it has been documented that such a woman will find herself attracted to someone other than her spouse—even to someone subjectively characterized as undistinguished in appearance and self-absorbed in personality. Perhaps it is this self-absorption that proves irresistible to our hypothetical professional as she approaches a hypothetical middle age; perhaps, contrary to all of our earlier hypotheses, such a woman is looking for someone who does not need or desire her in any other than a physical way. Perhaps this quality attracts her precisely because, on some level, she wishes she shared it. But here we come close to reducing attraction, infinite in its variety, to a single formula. In understanding what animates erotic desire, we are no closer than were our ancestors, who looked for their answers to the stars.

29 *Members of this dying breed may bear little resemblance to one another. In the wild, however,* Integrity *recognizes its own by the strong jaws and sharp eyes endemic to the species.*

SEE ALSO:
(014) CONSENSUS   (020) DISCRETION   (022) DIVORCE
(026) FAMILY VALUES   (032) FREEDOM   (036) GRAVITY
(074) MIDLIFE CRISIS   (106) SACRIFICE   (122) VULNERABILITY

INTIMACY

This would be right after the first time they went all the way. Which, just so you know, was Lacey's first time ever. It was the year after her dad had died all suddenly like that; her mom was going to the city for the day. "You're in charge, Lacey," Mrs. Hungate had said—as if that cretin of a little brother of hers would ever let her tell him what to do. Plus when Gabe was around it wasn't like Lacey had a whole lot of attention left over for anyone else, you know? Picture Lying Tommy telling her he's going to the library or to volunteer at the orphanage or whatever and then slipping off to do whatever it was he was really doing. Lacey is alone, except for Gabe there with her in that totally amazing house her dad paid for. He's just been inside her. She hasn't loved it, exactly, but she loves him, and now they're lying together with the fall light, that totally clear morning sunlight that comes off the Sound filling up the lace curtains she's pulled so no one can see in, and all of a sudden, boom, he's totally there. He's propped up beside her and he's fixed her in his eyes like he never does with anyone else. It's what she lives for, she'll tell me, that look like he can see right down into you. (As if I would ever have any idea what she was talking about. As if he would ever turn that look on me.) Anyway, he moves. She thinks he's reaching for another condom from the nightstand, but really he's grabbing that Sharpie he always carried, and before she can say anything he's drawing a bird freehand on her upper arm, a hawk I think. And in its claws a heart. Not a valentine heart but like with veins and everything. I know, I know, she showed it to me afterward and I was like, can you get any lamer. But secretly I was jealous. That became their thing, I guess, because sometimes after practice, when the locker room had emptied out, I would catch a glimpse of her all alone in the shower stall, with these wild designs all done in marker on the hidden spaces of her abdomen, the ones that don't show when your clothes are on. And whatever those bitches told her later, he never brought out the Sharpie for me, which is how I knew we'd made a mistake.

30   *By day, this creature lies motionless near watering holes, where the noise and movement of larger beasts will distract potential predators. Only when night falls does* Intimacy *awaken and begin its search for sustenance.*

IRONY

The new linoleum was the last of the improvements they made to the house that year, and after her son found her husband sprawled on it in the cardiac arrest that would end his life, Marnie wanted to rip it up with her bare hands. She wanted to never walk on it again. She blamed that linoleum, somehow. And she blamed herself, because when she'd called from the city that night to say she'd be getting home late from the alumni dinner and heard the answering machine pick up, she assumed he was out, rather than dying in the kitchen. He still went out often, for a man his age. She had no reason to feel guilty, there was nothing she could have done, was Elizabeth's take on things. During the first month of widowhood, Marnie walked over to the Hungates' nearly every night. But the conversations were like television. Afterward, she felt even more lonely. Marnie blamed her own inability to be honest about her feelings about Frank; not for a minute did she think that maybe it had something to do with Elizabeth.

31   *Thanks to modern biotechnology practices, traces of* Irony's *DNA are now present in the genome of almost all the other organisms that comprise the North American Family.*

LOVE

You'd seen him when they wheeled him in, you would've said forty-eight hours to maybe seventy-two at the outside. Even under the sheet on the gurney, you could tell from the way the fluids had begun to seep, like the way grease from a cheesesteak will turn the bag almost clear where it soaks through. Anytime you're talking about second- or third-degree, you're talking about a lot of fluid loss. That's the major danger. Think of a piece of meat that's been overcooked. That's all we are, really. Now you have Dr. Ross running around like the Queen of Spain because her case study's coming out in *JAMA*. And I'll give her credit for pioneering the technique—there's some who won't, but what do I know about it? But there's a big difference between keeping someone from dying and giving them a reason to live. And since that seems to be the point of your question, let me just mention his family and that little cheerleader who made the cookies. They were there every day when I came on, and she was there when I went off.

32   *Though hardly the most visible member of its kingdom,* Love *has never been as
endangered as conservationists would have us believe, for without it, the Family
would cease to function.*

SEE ALSO:
(012) COMMITMENT   (068) MATERNAL INSTINCT
(076) MOMENT OF CLARITY   (086) PARTINGS
(100) RECONCILIATION   (102) RESIGNATION   (126) YOUTH

MATERIAL

One house, two cars, four sets of clothes, gratuitous quantities of shoes, daily
medications, weekly groceries, glossy monthlies, a year's supply of firewood for
the wood-burning stove, a garage worth of tennis rackets and basketballs, a lifetime
of cigarettes. Honey can I, Daddy can't I, Dad why can't I, won't you, will you?
Please would you write a check, please can I have some cash, please could we
put your name down for a small donation? Of course Frank would. He can. He
could. For cell phones and PalmPilots and personal computers, he'd shell out.
For cornerstones and uniforms and Meals on Wheels for the elderly. These things
cost money, but then that's why he worked. In the end, well, it's always easier to
say yes.

33   *Although* Material's *impact on other species continues to puzzle observers, it has proven difficult for any ecosystem to flourish in its absence.*

SEE ALSO:
(004) ADULTHOOD   (024) ENTERTAINMENT
(030) FISCAL RESPONSIBILITY   (040) GUILT   (052) HOME
(078) MORTGAGE   (124) WHATEVER

MATERNAL INSTINCT

There's a plywood wall, six feet high by ten wide, in the backyard of the house occupied by Elizabeth and Jackie and, until recently (on Mondays, Tuesdays, Thursdays, and every other weekend, anyway), Gabe. Elizabeth had it built and, whatever happens to him, will never have it removed, because it is not hers to remove. Moisture off the Sound and extreme temperatures have faded the paint and warped the wood until it curls at the edges like paper. The figures, though, are still visible: faces, flags, birds, bodies, whorls, and jags and the name he chose to represent him, Casper, written over and over. Repetition is how he'd learned. She'd heard the bass booming from behind the closed door of his room. She'd seen the way he'd abandoned the GameCube, the way he stooped over his sketchpad. And she'd figured, at least he wasn't on drugs, as Marnie Harrison claimed half of the kids at the high school were. She'd figured, better under her own figurative roof than out somewhere doing God knows what, like Marnie's son. Gabe didn't have to thank her. The light in his face as he practiced his . . . what did he call them? . . . his throw-ups, his burners, was enough.

34 Maternal Instinct *hovers near the top of the food chain. Dominant females, who do the hunting for the herd, have been known to attack creatures as formidable as* Rebellion *and as insignificant as the smallest* Boredom.

SEE ALSO:
(002) ADOLESCENCE (016) CUSTODY BATTLE (018) DEPRESSION
(032) FREEDOM (074) MIDLIFE CRISIS (082) NATURE VS. NURTURE
(086) PARTINGS (094) QUESTIONS, NAGGING (098) RECOGNITION
(106) SACRIFICE

MATURITY

You know, Alphonse, things could be worse. Mom and Dad are talking again and the little tree we got him from the drugstore by the hospital makes the windowsill look less lonely, even though the thawing doesn't seem like December and I bet he's sad he's missing all the sunshine. Yesterday, Alphonse, he said his first thing since it happened, and do you know what? It wasn't to Mom or Dad or Lacey. It was to me. He reached out and grabbed my arm right here above the elbow and he said without moving his lips, "Don't ever grow up." I bet he would have been smiling if it didn't hurt to smile. Now you might be wondering what he meant by "Don't grow up," but I knew just what he was saying. He was saying, "Don't ever end up like me," and do you know what, Alphonse? I don't think I will!

35

More retiring than Adulthood, *with which it is routinely confused*,
Maturity *is associated with* Discretion, Grief, Resignation, *and* Sacrifice.

SEE ALSO:
(008) BOREDOM   (012) COMMITMENT   (056) INNOCENCE
(064) LOVE   (066) MATERIAL   (090) PRIVACY
(100) RECONCILIATION   (118) TRADITION

MEANING, SEARCH FOR

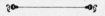

Tall tales Tommy told: that he held brown belts in tae kwon do and jujitsu. That his dad had let him drive the Porsche when he was only thirteen. That his IQ had been tested at 160. That Gabe Hungate was his best friend. That he and Gabe Hungate were half brothers, blood brothers. That Gabe Hungate had stolen his Roger Clemens rookie card. That he could make a fire by rubbing two sticks together. That he had once moved a spoon a couple inches across a table just by thinking about it. That he had lost his virginity in junior high, at sleepaway camp. That he and his dad went golfing every Saturday. That he had been born in Brooklyn. That he could play electric guitar and was getting one from his dad for his birthday. That his dad made over a million dollars per year. That his dad gave one quarter of his income to charity. That his dad secretly worked for the CIA. That his mother was the former Miss Sheepshead Bay. That his sister was adopted. That he was trying out for linebacker. That he would inherit ten million dollars when he turned eighteen. That he wasn't high right now. That he had already been accepted at Harvard on account of his precocious SAT scores. That any of this would have mattered, if that was actually his dad buried out there in the cemetery instead of the dummy his dad used to fake his own death before slipping away to Brazil on a top-secret mission the gravity of which only Tommy, his sole confidant, understood.

3b

Although the Search for Meaning *is one of the most commonly occurring organisms in the North American Family, identifying it is complicated by its ability to mimic other species, such as* Infidelity *or* Material.

SEE ALSO:
(006) ANGST   (026) FAMILY VALUES   (034) FRIEND OF THE FAMILY
(040) GUILT   (048) HIERARCHY   (054) INFIDELITY
(092) PROVIDENCE   (098) RECOGNITION   (114) TANTRUM
(120) UNCERTAINTY   (124) WHATEVER

MIDLIFE CRISIS

One of those backyard barbecues toward the end of summer. A season of short-ening days, when the specter of school hangs nearby, daring the kids to name it, to make it real. A season when Japanese lanterns have again become de rigueur. When if, like Elizabeth Hungate in one of her sudden and misguided fevers of trying to change her life, you've had your son drag the moldy box of Japanese lanterns from the garage out to the curb, you might curse yourself: you should have known you'd only have to buy them again. After all, everything comes back eventually. Haven't you witnessed this scene before: the sway of the little colored lanterns in the pool's unquiet surface? The drone of the air conditioner at the side of the house? The yapping dog next door? The cluster of patio chairs the adults have drawn together and abandoned like toys on the lawn while Jack flips the burgers and Marnie goes to make sure Tommy and Gabe are getting along and Frank goes inside to mix more drinks? Elizabeth has been here before. Returning from the bathroom, she's paused at the sliding back door, close enough to feel the cool radiating off it. The lightning bugs are out. Gabe floats nonchalant in the pool, fully clothed, his shorts bloated with an air-bubble. He's gesturing rudely to Lacey, who's just pushed him in. Lacey she doesn't know about, but Elizabeth can see that beneath her son's merciless teasing, he is already half in love with the girl, and it hurts her with a sharpness that almost stops her breathing. Here's another hurt: though she doesn't want to, she can feel Frank standing behind her. She wishes she could melt into the glass, become transparent too, a thing people only notice in passing. She wants to tell Gabe never to fall in love. But she won't. Besides: he always has to learn everything the hard way.

31   *An erratic* Maturity *pattern characterizes the* Midlife Crisis: *it may remain a manageable size for years, only to reach its full stature in a few turbulent days.*

SEE ALSO:

(004) ADULTHOOD   (020) DISCRETION   (022) DIVORCE
(026) FAMILY VALUES   (036) GRAVITY   (058) INTEGRITY
(068) MATERNAL INSTINCT   (082) NATURE VS. NURTURE
(086) PARTINGS   (122) VULNERABILITY

MOMENT OF CLARITY

⚬━━━━━⚬

What the fuck have we been doing with ourselves?

38

SEE ALSO:
(056) INNOCENCE   (102) RESIGNATION

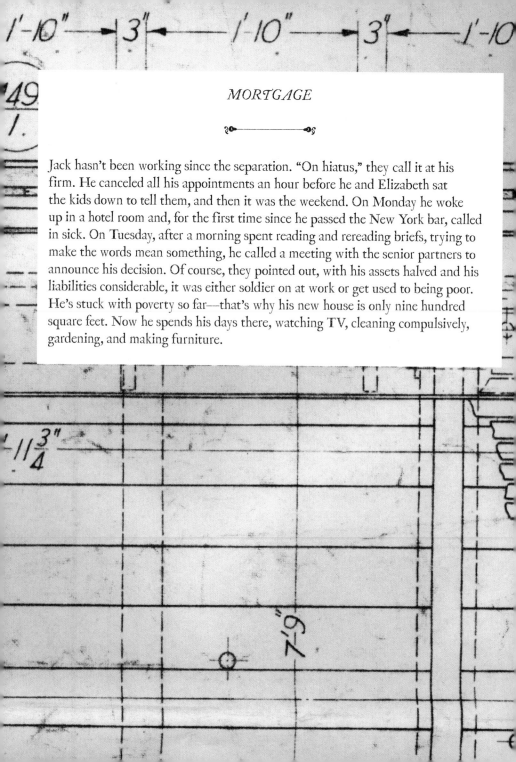

MORTGAGE

Jack hasn't been working since the separation. "On hiatus," they call it at his firm. He canceled all his appointments an hour before he and Elizabeth sat the kids down to tell them, and then it was the weekend. On Monday he woke up in a hotel room and, for the first time since he passed the New York bar, called in sick. On Tuesday, after a morning spent reading and rereading briefs, trying to make the words mean something, he called a meeting with the senior partners to announce his decision. Of course, they pointed out, with his assets halved and his liabilities considerable, it was either soldier on at work or get used to being poor. He's stuck with poverty so far—that's why his new house is only nine hundred square feet. Now he spends his days there, watching TV, cleaning compulsively, gardening, and making furniture.

39   *Many prospective owners adopt this difficult beast as a first step toward the housebreaking of* Security.

SEE ALSO:
(016) CUSTODY BATTLE   (020) DISCRETION   (032) FREEDOM
(052) HOME   (066) MATERIAL   (100) RECONCILIATION
(106) SACRIFICE   (118) TRADITION

MYTHOLOGY

The class spent much of December constructing the N.A. Village. The teacher painted a tarpaulin green to represent Land, leaving a blue margin of Water. There was perfectly good land and water beyond the window of the classroom, Jackie wanted to say, but she was called back to help construct Trees from rolled cardboard and tissue paper, and by the time they moved on to Crops, she'd forgotten. Pumpkins made of modeling clay, cornstalks fashioned from pipe cleaners, tiny clay gourds on pipe cleaner vines with tissue paper leaves . . . Crops took forever. Jackie put hers near the Water, for ease of irrigation. Longhouses were easy enough; everyone brought in a shoebox. They spent a day cutting construction paper bark to cover the logos and shoe sizes. The completed Houses were arranged in a circle, not like the Wagons they'd made in the Pioneers unit, but facing in, toward the center of the Village, where the tribal council would meet. People and Animals came last. People: clothespins colored brown, yarn hot-glued on for hair, felt tunics and tools made of toothpicks. Animals: more modeling clay. People went in the Village and Animals went in the Forest. For protection, Jackie erected a Popsicle-stick Stockade. When she leaned down so her head was almost level with the carpet, what she saw was another world. She imagined the People and Animals moving around at night, preparing for an ambush, ravaging the classroom in the dark. Then, a few days before Christmas break, the class gathered in a semicircle around the Village. "Don't touch," the teacher said. "This is a solemn occasion." She passed out notecards marked Trees, People, and Animals. "Jackie, what did I just say?" she said. "A very solemn occasion. You see, this is the world in which the N.A.s lived. Before the Europeans came and razed the Trees. Tree people, come forward," she said. Kids with Trees notecards were told to remove the Trees from the tarpaulin. "Without the Trees, where did the Animals go?" Jackie asked. The teacher nodded. "Very astute. Animals people, remove the Animals. Without Animals, the People had no source of food. No, they couldn't eat the Europeans, don't be silly. People people . . ." Jackie stood up. Outside, it was winter. The playground was a big, white blank. Already, she could see how it all would stretch away. Uninhabited, the Longhouses would crumble. Sans Houses, Crops, People, Animals, and Trees, only a flat expanse of canvas would remain. And by the end of school, kids would be back in the cubby area staging miniature wrestling matches between the clothespin N.A.s they'd made. They would be reminded to take home their People and Animals, but they would forget, and then they'd get left here: broken Indians, some deer, and a Tree on the muddy floor of the cubby area, everything they'd worked so hard on waiting to be thrown away. She pretended not to feel the other kids staring at her as she began to pluck the Longhouses off the tarpaulin. She pretended not to hear the teacher say, "Jackie? What on earth are you doing?"

40   *Without* Mythology, *what would protect the Family from the elements?*
Experiments designed to answer this question have so far proved disastrous.

SEE ALSO:
(056) INNOCENCE   (126) YOUTH

NATURE VS. NURTURE

It's tough to say in retrospect whether it was the divorce that made him reckless. He can remember tightrope-walking the third-story beams of a house under construction in the neighborhood years ago. He can remember Lacey yelling at him to come down, and Lying Tommy standing yards behind her, just watching, as though waiting for him to fall. Maybe it was genetic, although if anyone was a by-the-book player it was his dad. But maybe he got it from his mom. Maybe the divorce had just drawn out his latent tendencies in that direction, sent him spinning out past the point of acceptable risk. But then there was Lacey. So maybe it was when he got mugged that time at the LIRR station. There's something liberating about realizing that you can stare into the black hole of a handgun and still feel nothing. Because it was only afterward that he began to court disaster in earnest. That he began to turn off the headlights in the middle of the highway. That he graduated from bombing municipal walls around the county to sneaking into city trainyards in the dead of night. It was easy, with his mom and dad not talking. You just told each parent you were with the other. It was almost like freedom, except that nothing gave him pleasure anymore, except the trains. So maybe it was that, the incident with the gun. Whatever the case, he doesn't feel fearless anymore. Because it's not death you ultimately have to worry about. It's pain.

41   *The exact character of this unlikely hybrid has puzzled Family-watchers for years.*

OPTIMISM

Marnie pads barefoot into a cold kitchen and lights the burner underneath some water. Her first few attempts have been disasters: whites dissolving, little wisps of yolk reaching out for the walls of the pot. Frank's away on a golfing junket, and last night, on the phone, she almost gave in and told him. His teaspoon of vinegar hasn't helped. This is the way we talk when he's on the road, she thinks. I confess my failings, and he gets to tell me everything I'm missing, everything I'm doing wrong. She cracks the egg into a small bowl, careful not to break the yolk. Even two years later, he won't talk about it. The burner's blue crown hums in the predawn dim. She reaches for a wooden spoon. Bubbles rise like loosed balloons toward the surface as she stirs. A pang in her abdomen. When Frank used that word, centripetal, it made her think at first of her father's desk chair, the leather one that revolved on casters. As a little girl, on trips to his office downtown, she had climbed into it with her dolls. She had spun around and around, her shoe scuffing the wall. The G-force made her feel like an astronaut. But hadn't it pulled her outward, until she felt she would, at any second, fly off? "Trust me," Frank said. He calmly explained that that had been an illusion. It was just centripetal force, he said, combining with the first law of motion to create the feeling you were being pulled away from the center. Now Marnie tips the egg into the centrifuge of water. She takes a breath. She reaches beneath her nightgown and places a hand on the taut space beneath her navel, where their first child, finally, is growing. "Trust me," he said. Centripetal literally means center-seeking. She is slightly disappointed to discover that he's right. The center does hold. In the midst of all that boiling water, the egg's innards spin like a tiny, soft sun. So why does her universe feel smaller today? It might have been their little boy's birthday, had she carried him to term. Blue balloons. You weren't supposed to tell anyone until three months in. She had broken that rule then, but now she knows better. Another month will pass before she'll tell Frank. She wants to be certain. But she already has a name picked out. Funny, she thinks (though he undoubtedly would have reminded her that funny wasn't what she meant, exactly). Here I've been telling myself everything was falling apart, when I just didn't realize what I was falling toward was the center.

42 Optimism *lives so long as to seem, to the human observer, practically immortal—but unlike that of other creatures, the development of* Optimism *proceeds in reverse. That is,* Optimism *is enormous at birth, and gradually shrinks to its adult size.*

SEE ALSO:
(004) ADULTHOOD   (014) CONSENSUS   (018) DEPRESSION
(034) FRIEND OF THE FAMILY   (048) HIERARCHY   (052) HOME
(062) IRONY   (066) MATERIAL   (110) SECURITY

PARTINGS (AMICABLE AND ACRIMONIOUS)

The look on his face, his beautiful face that beneath the bandages was now yellow, green, and gray, a raw scar. The high-pitched sound that came from his mouth when she entered his field of vision. The closing of his eyes, the tightening of the mouth. The nurse had to give him another shot of Demerol so that he would relax his face. This was how any mother would feel. She should never have encouraged the graffiti. Inside, she was collapsing, like a sail split from top to bottom, but she told herself she couldn't show weakness. Instead she placed her hand on top of his bandaged head, with no more weight than a thought. She said, "Oh, honey." She said, "I love you. I'm here. I love you." She willed him to hear it, to take to heart these words, a depth of feeling she hadn't experienced since his birth. She hadn't noticed Jack come in, and jumped a little when she felt his arm around her shoulder. She didn't open her eyes or cease her murmuring or shake him off. She could feel his chest rising and falling against her upper arm, and she leaned her head against it, lightly, willing to believe, for a moment at least, that this was what it was there for.

Locked in Sibling Rivalry, *the two subspecies of* Parting *are unable to coexist peacefully. However, despite the characteristics that distinguish the two, each is capable of mutating into the other over time.*

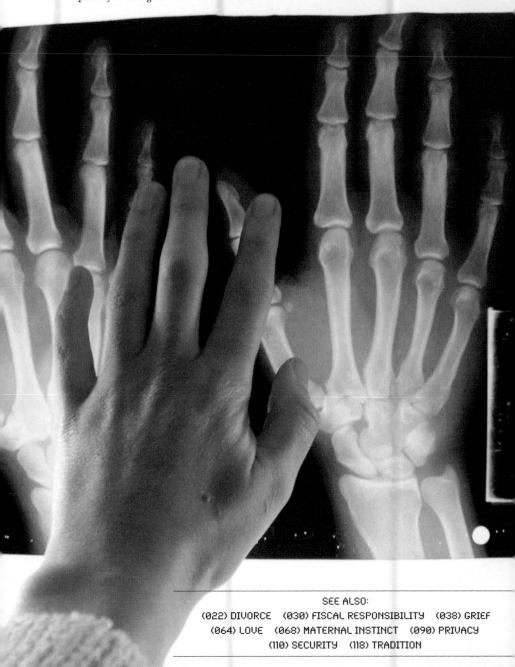

SEE ALSO:
(022) DIVORCE   (030) FISCAL RESPONSIBILITY   (038) GRIEF
(064) LOVE   (068) MATERNAL INSTINCT   (090) PRIVACY
(110) SECURITY   (118) TRADITION

PHASE

Once upon a time in a faroff Kindom there lived a girl named Jacqueline. Her father was king, her mother was queen, and her brother was prince more offen than not, which made her a princesse. Princesse Jacqueline loved to talk, tell jokes and pritend to be a monkey. One thing this princesse did not love was to be a lone. They were charmed by her way with a story and her monkey dance and put up with her fear of solotude. Given a choise, who would chuise to be a lone? But a bewichment began to fall over the land, so graduelly the princess can't tell you exackly when it started. First, her brother, the prince, got a mosterious illnesse. He began to keep secrets and send her away when she nokt on his door. Then the queen and the king didint love each other eny more and they split the kingdome in 2. Princesse Jacqueline found herself under a spell that trapt her in a glasse box, so even when she could see there were peepul a round her, they couldn't ~~hear man~~ hear her. The princesse grew very angry. Sometimes she would bang her hands against the glass. Sometimes she would screme, because she had read that certin high notes could brake glass. The childrin of the land grew fearfull of her, because they thot this was the way she was allways. Even at her most dispairing, tho, the girl new in her heart that the spell would be broken someday, and that she would live happily ever after, because that was the way it happened in evry story.

44 *With their keen senses,* Youth *are more apt to recognize that they have encountered a wild* Phase *than are adults.*

SEE ALSO:
(008) BOREDOM   (032) FREEDOM   (056) INNOCENCE
(100) RECONCILIATION   (112) SIBLING RIVALRY

PRIVACY

When the nurse came in at the end of her shift to change the bedpan and replace the IV bags, the girl had vanished like a night spirit, leaving behind only a chair pulled close to the bed, a welter of crumpled tissues, and an unfinished crossword puzzle. The patient, for his part, was still asleep. The hand on top of the blanket was unburned, a child's hand. She turned it gingerly over to check that the needle was secure and was surprised to find, inked on the palm, a messy blue heart, the Valentine's kind. The next afternoon, during his sponge bath, she would be careful to avoid this area, as it seemed to mean something to the patient.

45   *Experts disagree about whether this fragile organism is rapidly vanishing from the landscape or merely evolving into a hardier species.*

SEE ALSO:
(012) COMMITMENT   (028) FIDELITY   (036) GRAVITY
(038) GRIEF   (044) HABITS, GOOD   (060) INTIMACY
(064) LOVE   (070) MATURITY   (116) TENDERNESS

PROVIDENCE

That winter, shortly before the string of break-ins in the big shoreside houses came to its abrupt end, The Honorable Robert Perlmutter was awakened from a nap on the leather couch in his study by more barking and the creak of the kitchen doors below. Had he been more alert, he might not have shouted "Hello?" but in his half-waking state some part of him was convinced it must have been one of the neighbor boys returning home from school. Hearing nothing else, he rose. His arthritis spiked as he crossed the room to the window. He remembered that his own boys were grown, and gone, and that his only daughter still lay where he'd said goodbye to her twenty-eight years earlier, in a graveyard under the flight paths to LaGuardia. He remembered that one of the neighbor boys was in intensive care. He remembered the crime report in the paper. And he was surprised when he saw the flash of pale neck on the figure sprinting toward his hedge. Justice was blind and so forth, but he'd just assumed that the prowler would be a Negro.

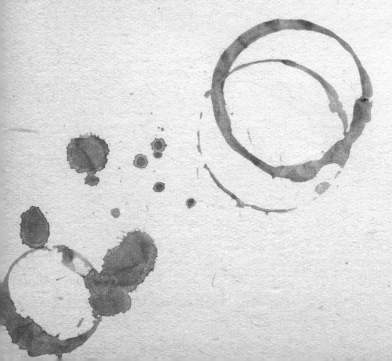

46   *Skeptics have long dismissed* Providence *as a figment of* Mythology, *and yet sightings—always in the wilderness, always uncorroborated—persist.*

QUESTIONS, NAGGING

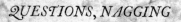

Who did Elizabeth sleep with?
What does Lacey see in that boy?
Why "Casper"?
Is there life after death?
What is Jackie doing in this story?
Why does anyone smoke cigarettes?

47   *These household pests have plagued the Family throughout its history, proving*
      impervious to radiation and other forms of Security.

REBELLION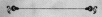

A lark at first, squirreling through the opening where the storm fence didn't quite reach the ground. Telling myself I only wanted to know I could do it if I wanted to, just like when I had Michelle DuPlessis flirting in the parking lot outside the gym instead of inside cheering with Lacey. I didn't really mean for anything to happen. But then why had I cased the perimeter four times before, looking for a way in? Why had I brought my backpack and the pocketful of good caps? Why did I let her go down on me in the dark behind the windshield? No one ever tells you there's such a thing as a sad blowjob. And the truth is it's never enough, nothing's ever enough, except bombing my name in wet red letters onto the side of a side-railed car, top-to-bottom burning, when everything evaporates but the hiss and the smell of paint. Everything but myself, all alone out here where the arcs of the nearest security lights don't quite overlap.

48   Rebellion, *common to every habitat, aids the long-term functioning of the Family by clearing out the dead and dying.*

RECOGNITION

Tommy had been a straight-A kid when the boy two doors down was making his way methodically through his parents' neglected liquor cabinet, drinking the bottles down halfway and filling them back up with water. And when, in the summer after his eighth-grade year, he tried once more to ingratiate himself with the older boy, the idol of his youth, Gabriel saw right through Tommy's stories about summer camp, about smoking weed, about eating some mushrooms once— not a lot, but enough that he thought he might have started to see visuals. It began to seem to Tommy that he, who worked harder at school and was bigger and stronger and, at least on paper, smarter, deserved some acknowledgment, and so what if he bent the truth sometimes? But poor, troubled Gabe was the older one and got the girls and the attention, which beat trophies and grades as soundly as rock beats scissors. And when their families fell apart, within a season of each other, it was Gabe who got the sympathy, and the bribes from his oblivious mom and dad: the car, for example, and the applause for how well he was taking everything. When Tommy made up a little white lie about how his late father had discovered the Supremes, people recoiled in disgust. When Gabe wanted to vandalize walls, they built him a wall to vandalize. And when he broke into a trainyard and got what he had coming, he was tragic, romantic, a victim. And if he had died that night, Tommy knew, the dead kid would still have been the winner in the great attention sweepstakes, even if the living one had nailed himself to a cross. By that point, Tommy had nearly stopped going to class, and whatever time wasn't spent testing the locks of neighborhood backdoors and the credulity of pawnshop owners was wasted hotboxing cars in the lot behind the C-Store . . . as though his real life were nothing more than an attempt to catch up with his fictional one. Pot, at least, would have been something the two boys had in common, except that Gabe had already said goodbye to all that, and moved on to somewhere further out of reach.

49   Recognition *and* Sibling Rivalry *seldom share territory.*

RECONCILIATION

Jackie's in the waiting area with her lion, rubbing his fur, frowning to herself, when her dad appears at the end of the hall. They haven't spoken in a week and a half. That's not out of the ordinary these days, but bears mentioning because otherwise Jack might not feel so peculiarly moved by the sight of his daughter stroking a toy he'd picked out for her so many Christmases earlier, might not feel a fist forming in his chest. Immediately the awkwardness of seeing each other again after so long a silence evaporates. He's never felt more like a father than he does now, striding down the corridor toward her, folding her into his body with one crooked arm, kissing the top of her head, calling her "sweetie." "Hi, sweetie," he says. She says her mom's in there already.

50   Reconciliation *migrates to landscapes ravaged by* Grief *and* Partings.
By feeding on the carrion these predators leave behind, it encourages the
regeneration of fauna.

SEE ALSO:
(008) BOREDOM   (016) CUSTODY BATTLE   (020) DISCRETION
(064) LOVE   (070) MATURITY   (078) MORTGAGE
(088) PHASE   (118) TRADITION

RESIGNATION

The sole source of Gabe's charisma was that he'd never much cared what anyone thought, one way or the other. About his car, for example, the little piece-of-shit Geo they would have laughed out of the parking lot at school if they thought it would have bothered him. About his unlikely conversion to sobriety. Or about the threadbare clothes from before the divorce, which he continued to wear even after a growth spurt had put an inch between the cuffs of his pants and the tops of his shoes. But when, having stumbled onto the third rail, he felt the electricity light up his body in a flash of something as close to rapture as to pain, it occurred to him in a strange moment of detachment that, if God granted him life beyond this interminable burning, he would care a great deal about how he looked to other people.

51   *Thriving in climates too damp for its cousin* Rebellion, Resignation *is of uncertain value for the Family: neither predator nor prey,* Resignation *drains resources without contributing anything definite to the food chain.*

SEE ALSO:
(002) ADOLESCENCE   (006) ANGST   (018) CHEMISTRY
(022) DIVORCE   (036) GRAVITY   (086) PARTINGS
(096) REBELLION   (124) WHATEVER

RUMOR

Supposedly Lying Tommy heard it from Sketchy Dan one afternoon behind the C-Store. For a liar, Tommy tended to take what other people said pretty much at face value. They were chasing down handfuls of Jaz-X Junior ephedrine pills with rum and Mountain Dew and waiting for a buzz to hit. School had just let out, and they were watching kids pass in and out of the smudgy glass doors through the windows of the Sketchmobile. Lying Tommy had turned old enough to drive a year ago but still didn't have a car, I heard because his mom didn't trust him behind the wheel. Who would have? Anyway, Tommy said sort of wistfully, hey, there goes my neighbor. And Sketchy Dan said dude, that's the dude I saw getting his knob polished by Michelle DuPlessis outside the basketball game last week. Sounds like a freak coincidence if you ask me, but then, these things usually are.

52   Rumor, *a resilient parasite, feeds on the* Secret *until its host is destroyed.*
In agricultural areas, Discretion *is sometimes employed as a check on the*
Rumor *population.*

SEE ALSO:

(028) FIDELITY   (038) GRIEF   (040) GUILT

(054) INFIDELITY   (096) REBELLION   (098) RECOGNITION

(114) TANTRUM

SACRIFICE

Jack found it one day among the ailing tomato plants, probably as long as a man's arm . . . probably someone's pet, escaped or abandoned. It had hollowed out a hole several feet deep beneath the groundcover gone wild at the end of the backyard. Strangely, he didn't find himself repulsed. He kneeled, transfixed by the jade-colored body breathing slowly beneath the green. Later, he investigated on the Internet. *Uromastyx aegyptus*. It got to where, on sunny days when he sat on the back porch drinking domestic beer and pondering the wreck his life had become, the lizard would come near enough to be touched. It would dart away if he moved to hold it, but somehow just touching the ridge along its spine was enough. The lizard's little claws were oddly like human hands. Winter came, and the pallor of the belly began to spread across the jade-green body. Knowing the lizard wouldn't make it through December, he called animal control. A gloved arm reached into the hole and pulled the desperately scrabbling *Uromastyx* out. He thought of Gabriel, of the delivery room. He found himself holding the lizard, finally, making awkward little talk with the woman from animal control. And he found himself sobbing when the truck pulled away. He wasn't quite sure why. It was only a lizard, after all.

53   *In its rare appearances,* Sacrifice *may dazzle observers with the delicacy and beauty of its coloration.*

SEE ALSO:

(012) COMMITMENT   (020) DISCRETION   (052) HOME
(064) LOVE   (074) MIDLIFE CRISIS   (078) MORTGAGE
(084) OPTIMISM   (102) RESIGNATION

SECRET

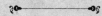

Lacey's was that she knew. Not immediately, but well before Tommy came to her with the story he'd heard from a, quote, reliable source. She knew as soon as she said it was a lie that it wasn't. Moreover, she knew why Gabe did it, and that she still wouldn't let him go. She kept it hidden, smothered the grenade with her body until the night he himself confessed, half undressed on the edge of her bed with its pink dust-ruffle, with its canopy. "I know," she told him. That, more than anything, she knows now, is what sent him running off that night, when he would end up in the hospital.

54   Secrets *breed rapidly. In concentration, they are the host organisms for* Rumor.

SECURITY

In light of all that's happened to these poor folks in little over a year, you have to be feeling pretty good looking around the dinner table at your own loved ones. Divorce and estrangement have never entered your home, nor has the misery of a prolonged hospitalization. And if death has touched you, well, you've all moved on. You can sit here in the dimmerswitch quiet long after the last sun has fled from the windows and enjoy a meal together, just the three of you. You can gaze on their faces, peaceably chewing, free from all but minor blemishes. Your son has slimmed down, you notice, and your daughter still looks healthy despite flaking on her cheerleading. And if their eyes are a little dark, it's because they worry, too, about the misfortune that can visit good people. After all, you've raised them right, cultivated in them the compassion so missing from everything these days. Or so you think, until your son opens his mouth.

55 *Security is prized by breeders for its handsome coat and protective disposition. When confined to small spaces, however, Security has been known to turn on its master.*

SEE ALSO:
(014) CONSENSUS   (018) DEPRESSION   (050) HOLIDAY
(062) IRONY   (080) MYTHOLOGY   (084) OPTIMISM
(114) TANTRUM   (120) UNCERTAINTY

SIBLING RIVALRY

Moms say they're supposed to take care of you, but this big brother is just not like that. He's mean. Like when I was in the living room and my mom was listening to her headphones and then my dad asked her if she had something she wanted to tell him and all of a sudden they were fighting, I went to the basement where my brother was. I was in second grade and he was in eleventh but he said go away. The lights were off. He was just sitting there. I could just hear his voice over the music, like a monster's in a cave. "I said go away," he said. So I went up to my room to say prayers, but I still remember that night, so anytime anybody tells me how lucky I am to have a big brother, I just think to myself no way. I'm the only one who cares about me. Well, and Alphonse, too, if you count Alphonse.

The Sibling Rivalry *hunts in groups of two or more. With its tremendous longevity, it may hibernate for years between periods of activity, though like species on other continents, this* Rivalry *tends to lose some of its vitality with age.*

SEE ALSO:
(006) ANGST   (008) BOREDOM   (022) DIVORCE
(024) ENTERTAINMENT   (070) MATURITY   (088) PHASE
(100) RECONCILIATION   (126) YOUTH

TANTRUM

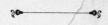

In an obscure way, I knew, it was my fault. If I hadn't told Lacey what I heard about Gabe, they wouldn't have fought. If they hadn't fought, he wouldn't have run out of her room, past my room, where I had been lying high with the lights off, trying to pretend not to exist. It was as though all of that garbage I had told that shrink after my dad died had suddenly and strangely come true. Of course, awareness didn't dawn on me immediately. It waited until the night just before New Year's when I made my mom cry by telling her that if she kept trying to ply us with turkey, to stuff us with ham, to silence us with roast beef, we would all end up like my dad. Walking through the frozen streets of the subdivision after that, I knew that the guilt was going to eat me alive, and from the inside. I knew, all of a sudden, that it would never stop as long as I stayed there, on the island where I'd invented my destiny.

An offshoot of the Rebellion *phylum, this toy breed is often found in domestic settings but has difficulty sustaining itself in the wild.*

SEE ALSO:
(018) DEPRESSION   (028) FIDELITY   (034) FRIEND OF THE FAMILY
(082) NATURE VS. NURTURE   (098) RECOGNITION   (104) RUMOR
(124) WHATEVER

TENDERNESS

They went to the museum that year mainly for the pleasure to be had coming out of the museum, when the world would return for a few minutes to what it was for the kids running up and down the steps: line and color, yellow spattering the oak branches even in winter, the lurid red of a subway globe thrust like a lollipop into the spittle-pale sky. Later they'd cross the park to catch a B or C down to Penn Station, and once, at some point somewhere in the middle where the buildings all but disappeared, he showed her how to see like an impressionist. "You've got to squint, Lacey," he said. "No, like this." There was a point (Frank insisted) at which the green would pop out. Are you there? Do you see it? Because having a daughter had made him feel for a while like it was possible to be restored, to see the world without the edges he'd grown accustomed to imagining were there. Because he knew they both needed to believe in restoration, in the days when they still went to museums.

58   *The wild* Tenderness *is less resilient than* Love; *without meaningful intervention, it will likely be extinct by the year* 2030.

SEE ALSO:
(012) COMMITMENT   (036) GRAVITY   (060) INTIMACY
(074) MIDLIFE CRISIS   (090) PRIVACY   (100) RECONCILIATION

TRADITION

Every year when the kids were small we allowed them to open one gift on Christmas Eve. I'd almost forgotten, until Jack stirred from his seat by the door and announced he'd be right back. He always was a sentimentalist—it was his idea that Gabe might like one of the frosted plastic Christmas trees they sold at the Walgreens across the highway; it was his string of colored lights waxing and waning in the sterile glass of the window. While Jackie continued to half-watch TV and half-watch her sleeping brother, I went to the window to follow Jack's progress across the parking lot. From the fourth floor, the grid of arc lights looked like netted pearls. Each time the Christmas tree dimmed, I could see the winter's first snow drifted around the curbs, cluttered with rocks and twigs but still faintly aglow. I could see the flicker of the highway through the barricade of trees, and beyond, the violet horizon, the lonely distant glimmer of an airplane climbing toward the clouds, a long-distance liner bound for Europe or California. When he reappeared in the doorway, he was holding the star. It had been his mother's before it had passed to us. Now for the last time it would top the family tree. Then it would pass to our son, if he lived to have a family of his own.

59   *It is common to find* Traditions *of many different shapes and sizes coexisting in a single habitat.*

SEE ALSO:

(050) HOLIDAY   (074) MIDLIFE CRISIS   (076) MOMENT OF CLARITY

(088) PHASE   (100) RECONCILIATION   (126) YOUTH

UNCERTAINTY

The carpet of the upstairs hallway is ghostly silent beneath my shoes, as if that were its purpose, not to make noise. Or maybe I'm still stoned and can't hear the fall of my own feet over the blah blah blah spilling from the TV in the kitchen, the barking dog next door. Behind the third door on the left is the bedroom where Gabe either is or isn't fucking my sister. I picture him giving it to her blankly, her head lolling back on the pillows. I picture Michelle DuPlessis with his dick in her mouth. I picture putting a pistol to his temple and saying, lie to someone now, motherfucker. The track lighting here has been waiting all its life to be this empty, this clinical, this distant. Lacey's room is quiet. Maybe they're sleeping. Maybe Gabe's not even here. Maybe she's not either; maybe the room is empty, and then what will I do with what I found out today? Will my big fat mouth stay shut? I have only to open the door to find out.

60   *The single most populous species on the North American continent,* Uncertainty *roams restlessly across the land, but in search of what, we cannot say.*

SEE ALSO:
(018) DEPRESSION   (034) FRIEND OF THE FAMILY   (054) INFIDELITY
(072) MEANING, SEARCH FOR   (096) REBELLION   (108) SECRET
(114) TANTRUM

VULNERABILITY

Though Jackie and her father had gone to see *The Lion King* on Broadway and Gabe was sleeping over at a friend's house, Elizabeth hadn't bothered to draw the blinds across the big sliding door at the back of the living room. The fluorescent light from the kitchen doorway made a white smear on the glass, beyond which everything was black rain. As she stood there, she imagined a murderer, a rapist staring back at her from the shadows of the backyard. She tried to tell herself she wouldn't care, that it didn't matter what happened. Still, she jumped a little when the doorbell rang.

cut

fold

Make your own book about a home. Tear out this page
carefully. Cut on the lines that say"cut". Fold on the
lines that say "fold". Put the pages together and ask
your mother or father to staple them.

cut

fold

WHATEVER

Last I heard, the Harrison boy next door was headed toward the expressway in a blue subcompact sedan. This was around the time the Hungate boy's little Geo disappeared from their driveway. (That eyesore graffiti next to their pool should have disappeared with it.) My Tiffany was the only witness to what happened to the Geo on the day it vanished, but what I heard was, the Harrison boy took it. There were a couple scenarios circulating at last month's Friends of the Library meeting, when Marnie Harrison didn't show up: first, that her son stole that car as some parting shot at the one in the ICU, whom he'd always felt mistreated by. Second, that he went to visit his friend at the hospital and confessed that he'd been the one to tell the girl the truth, and that the Hungate boy, no doubt heavily drugged, gave the Harrison one the car, after which the little turkey fled toward the city or points west, where for all I know he still is today.

This peculiar breed combines characteristics of Irony *and* Resignation *in a more compact frame. Impact studies on* Whatever *have yet to be undertaken.*

62

SEE ALSO:
(006) ANGST   (018) DEPRESSION   (028) FIDELITY
(032) FREEDOM   (040) GUILT   (066) MATERIAL
(070) MATURITY   (098) RECOGNITION

YOUTH

If you're listening, please make my brother get better. Whatever he did to deserve this, I bet it wasn't on purpose, and if you make him better I promise to go to church every Sunday from now on. Please take care of my mom and dad. Even if they're not in love anymore, if you would at least make them not mad at each other I will try to be better about visiting Dad. And Lacey has been really nice to my brother, nicer than I could be because it's hard for me to be nice and mad at the same time, so if you would make sure that something good happens to her then I will try to get all A's and B's on every report card left this year, which is only three but still, you've seen the other ones, you know. And look out for her family, while you're at it, or her mom and Tommy anyway—I don't know what happens to dead people. And everyone in our neighborhood and their pets. And all of the fish in the Sound. And all of Long Island and New York. And plus the kids in the Middle East on the news, and in Africa (the grown-ups, too). And everyone in hospitals all over the world, because, you might as well know, hospitals suck and smell bad. And everyone who lives where there's war or no money. And everyone who ever got hurt. Actually I guess you might as well bless all of the people, and the plants and animals, and Alphonse and all of the imaginary creatures and if there is life on Mars then the Martians, too. You keep your end of the deal, and I promise I will do my very best to be good at all times and also to make my bed every day (except when I forget), Creator Redeemer Sustainer Amen.

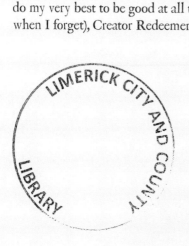

63   Youth *in full flight is a once-in-a-lifetime sighting; one can only hope rumors of its extinction are untrue.*

ABOUT THE PHOTOGRAPHERS

Jordan Alport ("Mythology") is an American director working in commercials, short films, and documentaries. www.thecolormachine.com/jordan-alport.

Timothy Briner ("Secret"), born in 1981, is an American photographer living in Brooklyn, New York. He is a member of the photography collective Piece of Cake. www.timothybriner.com.

Jessica Bruah ("Grief") grew up in Illinois and currently resides in Queens, New York. She received her MFA from the School of Visual Arts in 2009. www.jessicabruah.com.

Kara Canal ("Divorce") is an artist and educator living in Brooklyn. www.openstudiobrooklyn.com.

Sandy Carson ("Meaning, Search for") is a Scottish-born photographer and professional cyclist based in Austin, Texas. He has exhibited nationally and internationally and has published the monographs *Paradise Has Relocated* (2010) and *We Were There* (2016). His work has been published in *The New York Times*, *Aperture*, *The Guardian*, *Oxford American*, and *Juxtapoz*. www.sandycarson.com.

Alana Celii ("Uncertainty," "Youth") is a photo editor and photographer living in Brooklyn. She graduated in 2009 from Parsons School of Design, and has exhibited her work in the United States and abroad. www.alanacelii.com.

Janice Clark ("Hierarchy"), author of the novel *The Rathbones*, is a writer and designer living in Chicago.

Jason Curtis ("Intimacy") is an art director and photographer who resides in Portland, Oregon, after spending much of his life in New York City. He holds a degree in photography from the Pratt Institute. www.jasoncurtis.net.

John Paul Davis ("Reconciliation") is a poet, musician, designer, and programmer living in New York City. You can find out more about him, including publications and samples of his work, at johnpauldavis.org.

Chris Eichler ("Discretion," "Gravity," "Home," "Maturity," "Mortgage," "Privacy," "Security") has been photographing for more than fifteen years and has had documentary and fine-art work featured in a number of periodicals and galleries. www.chriseichler.com.

Amy Elkins ("Partings [Amicable and Acrimonious]") was born in New Orleans in 1979 and is now based in Greater Los Angeles. She received her BFA in photography from the School of Visual Arts, has published widely, and has had work exhibited at the Center for Creative Photography in Tucson, Arizona; the Minneapolis Institute of Art; and the Kunsthalle Wien in Vienna, among other museums. Her awards include a Light Work residency, the Aperture Portfolio Prize, the Villa Waldberta International Artist residency in Munich, and a Peter S. Reed Foundation Grant. www.amyelkins.com.

Jason Falchook ("Irony") is a Brooklyn-based photographer and a graduate of the Corcoran School of the Arts & Design. His photographs examine how we organize, live with, and experience the built environment. His work is in the permanent collections of the National Academy of Sciences and the U.S. Department of State, as well as in numerous private collections. He has exhibited nationally and internationally, including in group exhibitions at the Fort Lauderdale Museum of Art, the Corcoran Gallery of Art, the Katonah Museum of Art, and the Bronx Museum of the Arts. www.jasonfalchook.com.

Elizabeth Fleming ("Sibling Rivalry") is a photographer and social justice researcher who lives with her husband and two daughters in Maplewood, New Jersey. She received a BFA from Washington University in St. Louis, an MFA from the School of Visual Arts, and an MA in sociology from Columbia University. www.elizabethfleming.com.

Catherine Gass ("Vulnerability") is an adjunct assistant professor of photography at the School of the Art Institute of Chicago as well as the photographer for the Newberry Library. www.catherinegass.com.

Hans Gindlesberger ("Angst") lives and works in upstate New York. His projects, spanning photography, video, installation, and new media, have been exhibited at Galleri Image (Aarhus, Denmark); the Mt. Rokko International Photography Festival (Kobe, Japan); the Voies Off Festival (Arles, France); and FILE Media Art (São Paulo, Brazil). He has lectured nationally and internationally. Recently, his work has been published in *Diffusion*, *LensCulture*, and the *Flash Forward Tenth* anthology, published by the Magenta Foundation. www.gindlesberger.com.

Jonathan Gitelson ("Whatever") lives in Brattleboro, Vermont, and is an associate professor of art at Keene State College in New Hampshire. His work has been exhibited internationally and is in the permanent collection of institutions including the Museum of Modern Art; the Milwaukee Art Museum; the Museum of Fine Arts, Houston; and the Museum of Contemporary Photography. www.thegit.net.

Andres Gonzalez ("Adolescence," "Questions, Nagging") is a photographer, educator, and editor based in Vallejo, California. He has won awards from *Photo District News* and the Alexia Foundation and is a Fulbright Fellow. In 2012 he published his first monograph, *Some(W)Here*, to wide acclaim. www.andresgonzalezphoto.com.

Maury Gortemiller ("Habits, Bad," "Midlife Crisis") is an Atlanta-based photographer and educator. His work has appeared in exhibitions at the Museum of Contemporary Art of Georgia, the Atlanta Contemporary Art Center, and the Aperture Foundation Gallery in New York. He also writes on photography and contemporary art issues, most recently in *Art Papers*, *Perdiz Magazine*, and *The New Encyclopedia of Southern Culture* (University Press of Mississippi). www.maurygortemiller.com.

Jennifer Greenburg ("Resignation") is an associate professor at Indiana University Northwest. She has an MFA from the University of Chicago and a BFA from the School of the Art Institute of Chicago. Her work has been exhibited nationally and abroad, and solo exhibitions have been held at the Hyde Park Art Center and the Print Center, among other places. Her work is in the permanent collections of Light Work, the Museum of Contemporary Photography, and the Museum of Photographic Arts. Her monograph, *The Rockabillies*, was published in 2009. www.jennifergreenburg.com.

Ben Huff ("Integrity") is a photographer based in Juneau, Alaska. His book, *The Last Road North*, was published by Kehrer Verlag in 2015. He's currently working on a long-term project on the Aleutian Island of Adak and chasing smaller stories in the north. www.huffphoto.com.

Christy Karpinski ("Phase") was born and raised in Arizona. She currently teaches at Columbia College Chicago. www.christykarpinski.com.

Mickey Kerr ("Tradition"), born and raised in Kansas City, Missouri, is a commercial and fine-art photographer based in New York City. His work has been published and exhibited widely, including in a solo show at M.Y. Art Prospects gallery and in FlakPhoto's 100 *Portraits*. A graduate of the International Center of Photography, where he was a Sandy Luger fellow, he currently lives with his wife and daughter in Upper Manhattan. www.mickeykerr.com.

Liz Kuball ("Entertainment") is an editorial and commercial photographer based in Los Angeles. Her clients include *Dwell*, *Condé Nast Traveler*, *The New York Times*, *Monocle*, Ace Hotel, and Medium. Her fine-art work appeared in *The Collector's Guide to Emerging Art Photography* and has been exhibited across the United States and editioned through 20x200. www.lizkuball.com.

Michael Kwiecinski ("Adulthood") studied photography in New York City and now lives and works in Southern California. www.wondertribe.co.

Shane Lavalette ("Freedom," "Moment of Clarity") is a photographer, the publisher-editor of Lavalette, and the director of Light Work, a nonprofit photography organization in Syracuse, New York. www.shanelavalette.com.

Jason Lazarus ("Rebellion") is a Florida-based artist, curator, educator, and writer. Recent major exhibitions include solo shows at the Museum of Contemporary Art Chicago and Andrew Rafacz Gallery as well as *Black Is, Black Ain't* at the Renaissance Society, *About Time* at the San Francisco Museum of Modern Art, and *Michael Jackson Doesn't Quit, Part 3* at the Future Gallery, Berlin. Monographs on his work have been published by Light Work, SF Camerawork, and Illinois State University. He is currently an assistant professor at the University of South Florida. www.jasonlazarus.com.

Stacy Arezou Mehrfar ("Infidelity") has had work exhibited in the United States, Australia, Poland, and Germany, and her photographs are held in numerous public and private collections worldwide. Her first monograph, *Tall Poppy Syndrome*, was published by Decode Books, Seattle, in 2012. After living in glorious Sydney, Australia, for eight years, Stacy returned to her beloved New York City in 2016. www.stacymehrfar.com.

Nick Meyer ("Tantrum") lives and works in western Massachusetts. His first monograph, *Pattern Language*, was published in 2010 by Brick Publishing and his second monograph is forthcoming from Daylight Books in 2017. www.nickmeyerphoto.net.

Matt Nighswander ("Commitment") is a photographer and photo editor living in Brooklyn. He holds an MFA from Columbia College Chicago and has had solo exhibitions at Pictura Gallery in Bloomington, Indiana, and the Center for Fine Art Photography in Fort Collins, Colorado. His work has appeared in *The New York Times*, *Adbusters*, and the *British Journal of Photography*, and online at Time.com and the DailyMail.com.

He is patiently waiting for the public to demand the reunion of his postcollege band. www.mattnighswander.com.

Alexis Pike ("Sacrifice") is a sixth-generation Idahoan calling on the geography of her genes for inspiration. She currently lives in Bozeman, Montana, and is an associate professor at Montana State University. Her photography has appeared in *Harper's Magazine* and *Wired*. She has also been a Top 50 finalist for Critical Mass and has exhibited in the public art installation *The FENCE* and at Blue Sky Gallery in Portland, Oregon, which published a monograph of her work. www.alexispike.com.

Colleen Plumb ("Holiday") makes photographs and video and teaches at Columbia College Chicago. Her first monograph, *Animals Are Outside Today*, was published by Radius Books. She lives in Chicago with her husband and two daughters. www.colleenplumb.com.

Gus Powell ("Love," "Rumor") is a photographer and artist based in New York City. His monographs include *The Company of Strangers* and *The Lonely Ones*. www.guspowell.com.

Abby Powell-Thompson ("Innocence") is a film photographer residing in the Puget Sound area of Washington.

J. K. Putnam ("Chemistry") is a professional nature and landscape photographer based in Mount Desert Island, Maine, home of Acadia National Park. www.jkputnamphotography.com.

Shawn Records ("Nature vs. Nurture") holds a B.A. from Boise State University and an MFA from Syracuse University. His work has been shown widely and is in the permanent collections of the Museum of Contemporary Photography and the Portland Art Museum, among others. In addition to his artwork, he shoots commissioned assignments for publications including *Vice*, *Dwell*, *Travel + Leisure*, and *The New York Times Magazine*. He lives, photographs, and teaches photography in Portland, Oregon. www.shawnrecords.org.

Rebecca Blume Rothman ("Family Values") is a photographic artist, illustrator, and project manager who helps build big works of public art. She lives and works in Phoenix, Arizona. www.rebeccablumerothman.com.

Matthew Schenning ("Depression," "Fiscal Responsibility") is a Brooklyn-based photographer originally from Baltimore, Maryland, where he spent his youth playing in the abandoned spaces under highway overpasses. While seeking to understand his own relationship to his surroundings he interjects a bit of humor and poetry into the imagery of the everyday. www.schenning.com.

David Shulman ("Custody Battle," "Optimism") is a Brooklyn-based photographer and the co-founder of Boundless Brooklyn.

Kevin Sisemore ("Maternal Instinct," "Tenderness") is a photographer living and working in Kansas City. www.kevinsisemore.virb.com.

Brandon Sorg ("Providence") is a photographer living in New York City. www.brandonsorg.com.

Brian Sorg ("Recognition") has balanced a life of active work in both commercial and fine-art photography since completing his BFA at Columbia College Chicago in 2006. His photographs have appeared in more than fifty solo and group exhibitions and have been published in *Rolling Stone*, *XXL*, *Bloomberg Businessweek*, *ESPN the Magazine*, *Esquire Russia*, *Glamour France*, *L'Uomo Vogue*, and *Marie Claire*. www.briansorgfoto.com.

Sai Sriskandarajah ("Consensus," "Guilt") is a lawyer, artist, photographer, and tinkerer. He lives in San Francisco with his family. www.saisriskandarajah.com.

Tema Stauffer (frontispiece, "Boredom") is a Montreal-based American photographer whose work examines the social, economic, and psychological landscape of American spaces. Her work has been shown nationally and internationally, including exhibitions at the Sasha Wolf, Daniel Cooney Fine Art, and Jen Bekman galleries in New York and at the Smithsonian National Portrait Gallery. She was awarded an AOL 25 for 25 grant for innovation in the arts in 2010 for her work as an artist, curator, and writer. Stauffer is an assistant professor of photography at Concordia University in Montreal. www.temastauffer.com.

JJ Sulin ("Fidelity"), born in 1970, is a photographer who lives and works in Brooklyn. His work deals with the everyday. www.jjsulin.com.

Brian Ulrich ("Material") is an American photographer known for his exploration of consumer culture. Ulrich's work is held in collections including the Art Institute of Chicago and the Cleveland Museum of Art. In 2009 he was awarded a Guggenheim Fellowship. His work has been featured in *The New York Times Magazine*, *Time*, *Mother Jones*, *Artforum*, and *Harper's Magazine*. Aperture and the Cleveland Museum of Art published his first major monograph, *Is This Place Great or What*, in 2011. In 2013, the Anderson Gallery published the catalog "Closeout—Retail, Relics and Ephemera." www.notifbutwhen.com.

Consider Vosu ("Heirloom") lives and works in Portland, Oregon.

Grant Willing ("Friend of the Family") is an artist based in Brooklyn. He has exhibited his work in the United States and abroad, and has also self-published several books of his photographs and drawings on subjects ranging from black metal to citrus fruit. www.grantwilling.com.